"WHAT POSSIBLE REASON HAVE YOU TO CARE ABOUT ME AND MY FAMILY?" SHE SAID ROUGHLY.

It was his turn to feel stung by her words. "I have little choice when I observe a lone female of my acquaintance skulking off in the dead of night. Though you may not countenance it, I have *some* sense of honor!" Without thinking, he began shaking her. "If you ever do anything so idiotic again, I swear I shall—"

Alex snapped. He was hurting her, both with his grip and the truth of his words. Her hand shot out and delivered a resounding slap across his face.

Both of them were rendered speechless for a moment. Alex's mouth dropped in belated shock at what she had done. . . . Then his lips came down on hers, not tentatively, but hard and demanding. Alex stiffened in utter surprise, then found herself responding with equal passion.

She had never imagined a kiss could be like this. . . . Then he broke it off to run his lips down the inside curve of her throat.

"Don't ever scare me again like that, Alex," he murmured between caresses.

All at once, all the common sense that had dominated her life deserted her. She knew, beyond all doubt, that she must seize the moment. . . .

CODE of HONOR

ANDREA PICKENS

A SIGNET BOOK

SIGNET
Published by the Penguin Group
Penguin Putnam Inc., 375 Hudson Street,
New York, New York 10014, U.S.A.
Penguin Books Ltd, 27 Wrights Lane,
London W8 5TZ, England
Penguin Books Australia Ltd,
Ringwood, Victoria, Australia
Penguin Books Canada Ltd, 10 Alcorn Avenue,
Toronto, Ontario, Canada M4V 3B2
Penguin Books (N.Z.) Ltd, 182–190 Wairau Road,
Auckland 10, New Zealand

Penguin Books Ltd, Registered Offices:
Harmondsworth, Middlesex, England

First published by Signet, an imprint of Dutton NAL,
a member of Penguin Putnam Inc.

First Printing, July 1998
10 9 8 7 6 5 4 3 2 1

Printed in the United States of America

Chapter One

Even the slightest movement caused a grimace to pass over the well-chiseled features. One eyelid slowly pried itself open, then fell shut at the sight of a hazy but eminently recognizable bottle of brandy perched on the delicate gilt side table.

Good Lord, had he really polished off that one too?

With a groan he rearranged his long, muscled legs, only to find them entangled with a pair of much shorter, softer ones. A slender hand ran lightly over the dark curls of his chest, across the hard planes of his stomach, then roamed even lower.

"My lord," murmured a sultry voice. "It appears you are . . . awake. Quite awake." A pair of lips pressed against his shoulder, a tongue teased the tanned flesh.

Stifling another groan, he pushed her lush hips back into the satin sheets and rolled on top of her.

A half hour later, the Earl of Branford sat on the edge of the rumpled bed. The dull ache in his head only mirrored the one deep inside. After briefly massaging his temples, he finished pulling on his boots and then reached for his shirt.

"Must you go?" The raven-haired beauty let the sheet slip ever so slightly to bare one rose nipple.

The earl didn't even cast a glance her way as he essayed

to tie his cravat into some semblance of neatness. He stood up and, with a slight shake of his head, shrugged his broad shoulders into an impeccably cut coat of navy superfine. Reaching into one of the pockets, he removed a small box, exquisitely wrapped in embossed paper, and dropped it into the swirl of satin.

The lady unwrapped it. Her jaw tightened slightly as she draped the filigree gold bracelet winking with diamonds and emeralds around her wrist.

"It is indeed beautiful." After a moment of silence she added, "So this is good-bye?"

"It is time, Serena."

She gave a toss of her head, sending the dark ringlets cascading over her alabaster shoulders—even in anger, he thought cynically, she managed to look perfect.

"I suppose I should feel flattered that I've lasted longer than most of your mistresses."

"No, you should not. In fact, it is nothing personal." He straightened the gold signet ring on his little finger. "My banker will make the necessary arrangements, though with your charms, I doubt you will be without protection for very long."

"You are a hard man, my lord."

"Come now, my dear, do not play the injured party with me. You know very well you expected no less."

He turned and left the bedroom, quietly but firmly closing the door after him.

Outside, the raw chill slapped at his face. He turned up the collar of his greatcoat and settled the curly brimmed beaver hat on his long locks. At the corner his carriage was waiting. It was nearly four in the morning and though he was dead tired and feeling muzzy from the effects of the brandy and the boudoir, he couldn't face returning home. He rubbed a hand over his stubbly jaw, then rapped on the roof with the tip of his silver-chased walking stick.

"White's," he called out in his rich baritone. Then he settled back against the squabs and closed his weary eyes.

Despite the late hour, there was no dearth of activity at the exclusive club on St. James's Street. Gentlemen—many in far worse condition than the earl—were still at play in the gaming room while others nursed port or brandy in the comfort of the well-appointed rooms.

Branford handed his greatcoat to the porter and entered one of the main rooms. A hush fell over the small group of men gathered before the roaring fire. A number of wary eyes followed his progress as the earl made his way toward a vacant leather wing chair and ordered a bottle of claret to be brought posthaste. He settled his lanky frame into the soft leather and stretched his boots toward the warmth of the blaze. The wine appeared almost immediately. He poured a glass, but instead of raising it to his lips, he merely cradled it in his lap. His eyes fell half closed, an impenetrable look on his handsome features.

The frisson of tension eased. The buzz of conversation slowly began again as it became evident there was to be no immediate victim of the earl's sardonic tongue. Though some of those gathered there at that hour made up a rather reckless set, much given to heavy drinking, deep play, and short tempers, none cared to cross swords—verbal or otherwise—with a man of Branford's reputation.

"It's outside of enough," muttered one of the gentlemen by the fire, a middle-aged viscount with darting, ferretlike eyes set in an otherwise unremarkable face. "Is it true, Hammerton, that the chit behaved in such a manner? What is her aunt thinking of?"

"Her aunt is too busy with her nose buried in her late husband's writing to see beyond her spectacles. It's not like the girl has any prospects anyway. Why, she's as good as on the shelf—she must be at least three and twenty."

"What's she done?"

A stout gentleman, whose receding ginger hair would have given him the look of a monk were it not for the obvious effects of dissolution etched on his face, leered suggestively. "She went to view the statues that damned fellow Elgin brought back from Greece. Alone."

The man who had asked the question furrowed his brow. "Thought chits were allowed to look at art."

The ginger-haired man's leer stretched wider. "They are of horses and men. Buck-naked men."

A shocked gasp came from two of the group, but another of them, a baronet with the high shirtpoints and fussy waistcoat of a budding dandy, rocked his hips suggestively. "Likes horses does she? Perhaps she'd like a good mount."

There were guffaws all around. Another bottle of brandy was ordered. Emboldened by the response, the baronet took another long draught from his glass and continued. "You know these country gels. Her groom has probably been having at her. Wouldn't mind joining the sport myself, even though she's no diamond of the first water. Has spirit, though. Heard her arguing—*arguing,* for God's sake—with a man at the Haverly's rout. I like a filly with spirit between my legs."

"Aye, Vinley. It's well known you'd unbutton your breeches for *anything* that wears a skirt—"

"Enough!" A baron lately come down from his estate in Yorkshire, a newer member of their set, which included some of the less reputable members of the *ton,* scratched at his whiskers and looked slightly discomfited. He appeared to glance around the room as if to ascertain who was paying them any attention. "We are discussing, er, ladies, not some lightskirts from Southwark."

"Ah, but that is what makes it . . . interesting." The words came from an elegantly dressed man of medium height who was lounging against the mantelpiece. Toying with one of the many fobs that dangled from his embroidered waistcoat, he cast a surreptitious look at the figure of the earl, who seemed to be dozing, oblivious to the conversation.

"Would you think someone with a reputation of cutting a swath through the ladies—say, for example, Branford there—could get a forward girl like Miss Chilton to give him a tumble?" He picked for a moment at the edge of his immaculate cuff while some of the others traded nervous glances.

A young viscount drained his glass, swaying slightly in the process. "Aye, Hammerton. I'd put my blunt on Branford to have his way with her. Why, if all the rumors are correct," he added in a near whisper, "he's sampled the charms of half the wives of the *ton*—"

"Including yours, Fielding, for all the action you give her," jeered a voice.

"And welcome to the bitch he'd be," muttered the baronet as a flush rose over his face.

"I say it can't be done. The aunt's not that much of a loose screw, even if the chit is."

"A bet! A bet!" chorused two other voices, their tongues loosened by the copious amounts of alcohol consumed.

A ghost of a smile crept over Hammerton's lips. "What say you, Branford?" he called in a louder voice. "Care to partake in a little wager?" His tone conveyed a subtle tone of insolence.

The earl's eyes slowly opened, the flickering light catching a spark of sapphire. "What?"

"A wager," repeated Hammerton. "Care to bet on whether you can mount a certain lady?"

"Which lady?"

"One no better than she should be. Name is Chilton. Arrived from the country last week."

The earl stared at Hammerton from beneath hooded eyes.

"Now myself and Chumley are willing to wager it can't be done—in say, a fortnight. Anyone else with us?" A murmur of assent came from a few others. "So, Wilton and Chichester will join us. Say we each put up one hundred and twenty-five pounds. Do you care to match our five hundred pounds? With your vast fortune, it seems . . . fair." He emphasized the words "vast fortune" just enough to make his intent of doing so unmistakable.

A hint of emotion seemed to flash in Branford's eyes, but his face remained impassive. "It seems you do not tire of losing your money to me," he said evenly. "Over the last month we have been matched at cupping the wafers at Mantons, racing curricles to Bath, and running our horses at Ascot . . ." He let his sentence trail off deliberately. Hammerton's jaw tightened. "However," continued Branford, "if it amuses you to keep it up, why not?"

Hammerton swirled the brandy in his glass, suppressing the hot anger that welled inside of him. "I shall have it entered in the betting book."

"How will we have proof of who's won?"

The earl turned toward the voice. "Do you doubt my word?" he asked softly.

The gentleman shrank back a step. "Indeed, of—of course not, my lord. Stupid of me . . . must have had too much . . ." he trailed off lamely.

The matter was settled. The conversation drifted on to other topics. Hammerton took his leave and strolled out of the room, a faint but discernible look of satisfaction on his face.

"Aunt Aurelia! Alex! Cook is threatening to give notice if the two of you are late again for dinner."

A bespectacled nose peeked out from above a leather-bound quarto of *The Iliad.* At the other end of the table, a second appendage, liberally smudged with charcoal, looked up from a thick sketchbook. Two sets of eyes mirrored a vague surprise.

"I fear time has passed rather more quickly than I had imagined."

"My dear, it is *I,* at my age, who is supposed to say that." Lady Beckworth lay down her tome and patted absently at the neat bun of silver hair pinned at the nape of her neck. Her voice carried a tone of mild reproval, but there was a twinkle in her eye. Though age had brought the inevitable changes to her visage, it had not dulled the intelligence and life that radiated from the depths of their hazel color. There was, however, a glint of concern as she turned to face her niece. "You, on the other hand," she said lightly, "should be thinking about the Worthington's ball and not the leaf structure of *verbena patagonica.*

"Hmmmph." Alexandra Chilton closed her sketchbook with a little more force than necessary, then rubbed her hand absently on the folds of her muslin day dress, leaving a streak of gray down the side. "Why on earth should I be thinking about the Worthington's ball—I'm scarcely a giddy schoolgirl miss in my first Season. In fact, I'm as good as on the shelf . . ."

"Now, my dear—"

"Oh, Aunt, you know as well as I do it's the truth. I'm too old, too opinionated and too poor to attract any offer, decent or otherwise. And well glad I am of it. I've yet to meet a man who is . . . is interesting enough for me to want to be leg-shackled to him for the rest of my life."

"Alex, really!" Her aunt tried to look shocked, but her face dissolved into a grin and a chuckle escaped her lips.

"Oh, Aurelia. How lucky I am that I may freely express my sentiments and know that you, at least, will understand how I feel. And you have a . . . sense of humor as well. How awful not to be able to laugh at the foibles of Society—and one's self." She sighed. "My only regret is that we are such a burden on you. If I can find a publisher for my paintings on the flowers of Kent—and Mr. Simpson thinks it entirely possible—then I shall have an income and Justin and I can—"

Lady Beckworth had risen and come to stand by Alex. She placed a hand over her niece's. "Alex, you and Justin are a gift to me, hardly a burden."

Alex squeezed her aunt's fragile fingers but kept her face averted, afraid of becoming a watering pot, something she detested above all things in one of her sex. "Yes, well, it is Justin you should be concerned about," she said in a husky voice. "It is for his sake, after all, that we are spending a Season here. He deserves the chance to acquire a little town bronze and to convince Anne's father that he will make her a good match, despite his lack of fortune. So, I shall dutifully attend the Worthington's ball and try not to say or do anything too outrageous that might disgrace the family name—"

Another thump reverberated through the heavy oak door. This time it opened a crack as well, just enough to admit a slender young man with still a bit of coltish awkwardness about him. He ran his hand through his tousled sandy curls in mock despair. "The exact meaning of (ὀχηέω) and the number of stamens of *Nigella damascena* will have to wait until tomorrow," he announced in a light tenor, which struggled to sound deeper. But like his sister and aunt, his eyes danced with humor. He pointed a finger meaningfully toward the hall. "After you, ladies."

"Shall I put it all the way up, or let it fall like this?" It was the second time the question was asked.

"Oh dear, I fear I was woolgathering, Maggie. Let it fall, please." Lady Beckworth shifted in her chair as her longtime retainer continued to dress her hair for the coming evening. Though she gazed straight ahead at the large mirror on her dressing table, her eyes took in none of the details of her coiffure or her gown or even her own face, which was perhaps even more attractive than in her youth now that a strength of character had subtly shaped the pleasant features. Her thoughts were centered on her niece and nephew.

How capricious life was, she mused. To have lost her husband and her brother-in-law within weeks of each other was a cruel blow. But then Alex and Justin had come to live with her, the children she had never known. She hadn't thought it possible to feel true happiness again—she and her husband had, unlike many of the *ton,* had a marriage based on love and respect. But she had, in ways she had never imagined. Now, if only she could see both of them as happy as she was. Her mouth quirked in a rueful smile at such presumptuousness. She might as well wish for the moon, she knew, than to think she could control another's destiny. But to her, the two young people and their future were the most important thing in her life.

Justin must be a changling, so different from his father was he. Marcus had been a distant man, even before her sister had died, difficult to understand, especially when he retreated into his own private world of ideas. She shook her head slightly. She didn't think he really comprehended how much that forced his young, motherless children to fend for themselves, both emotionally as well as having to deal with the realities of keeping a household running, and with precious little funds to do it. Now nineteen, Justin had grown into a levelheaded young man who showed such a sense of responsibility for his family that she almost wished he would cut a caper or two, just to assure her he wouldn't lapse into priggishness. Perhaps that came from being the only male left of the family at age sixteen. But then she thought of his ready wit and warm laughter and she knew there was really no danger of that!

And he had ability too. He had applied himself to his studies at Oxford and his ideas on farming already had her small holdings turning a modest profit for the first time ever. She knew he was chafing at the bit to run a real estate. Any parent wise enough to look beyond the lack of title or fortune would find an unimpeachable husband for their daughter. And with his handsome features made even more appealing by his open, friendly manner, she did not doubt that there would be more than a few young ladies developing a tendre for him. However, he seemed to have his heart set on one, and with well-placed words here and there among her many connections, she hoped to be able to influence the girl's mother and father.

It was Alex she worried about. It was not that her niece lacked in practicality—if anything, she had too much of it, having had to have taken up the running of a household and the responsibility of a younger sibling at such an early age. It was Alex who learned to deal with tradesmen and stretch the meager budget when her father went haring off on his projects. No, it was that she was, well, she was too much like her father in other ways. Inquisitive to the point of pursuing an interest regardless of the consequences—Lady Beckworth thought once again of her brother-in law.

A brilliant naturalist, but in his passion to achieve his own goals, he had sacrificed certain things for his family that she wondered whether he had a right to do. And in the end, he had left them without a feather to fly with. Impetuous was another word that came to mind when thinking of both of them. Why else would Marcus have been rushing home on such a dismal night—no doubt to bring some fragile specimen back to his library—when no rational person would have attempted to drive a carriage along the seaside cliffs? Alex had that same unwavering determination, as well as the same touch of recklessness. She had acquired her father's love for the natural world and had translated it into becoming a botanical painter of no small talent. The only reason she had agreed to come to London was to meet the members of the Botanical Society, with whom she had been corresponding for several years.

A sigh escaped her lips. What a singular family they were, she herself immersed in finishing the work of her late husband, a translation of Homer's *Iliad*. But where she, at her stage and position in life, was allowed to be bookish and opinionated, Alex was in danger of being considered beyond the pale of Society with her attitudes. She was already considered old. Heaven forbid that she also get stuck with the reputation of being odd. Despite what the girl thought, Lady Beckworth was sure it would be a grave mistake for her niece to cut herself off from—

"I should think the red shawl, wouldn't you, Lady Aurelia?"

"Oh. Yes. Of course."

Maggie draped the soft cashmere over the slight shoulders and arranged it into neat folds. "You are late, as you well know," she said, speaking with the easy candor of a longtime retainer. "Now go along and enjoy the evening—

and don't you be worrying about those two. They will manage just fine."

Hammerton swirled his brandy, eyeing the rich amber color as his mouth turned upward at the corners.

"Don't know why you're looking so devilishly pleased with yourself," remarked his cousin. Arthur Standish turned his head as far as the starched, overly high points of his collar allowed. "Thought you, shall we say, disliked the Icy Earl. Can't imagine why you provoked such a wager with him." He paused to take a large swallow of his own drink. "Especially," he couldn't help but add, "since you've had precious little luck against him. He's bound to win this one too, given the dog's reputation in the bedroom. It's a wonder his breeches are ever buttoned."

Hammerton's mouth curled up even more. "Ah, but his conquest will serve my purposes very well. To have the girl disgraced and to have her family have to retreat back to the country is exactly what I want." A humorless laugh escaped his thin lips. "And to have Branford act as my unwitting pawn makes it even more sweet. A hundred and some odd pounds is well worth it to use him like a whore."

Standish grunted as he toyed with the numerous fobs dangling from his brightly striped waistcoat. "I say, it may be deuced clever of you. But I'd be very careful in voicing such thoughts aloud." He darted a glance around the room as he spoke as if to judge whether it was likely anyone could overhear them.

"I'm well aware of the fear most of you have of the man. Well I for one, do not hold him in such awe. I shall prove that his bloody lordship is not so clever by half as I am."

Standish frowned. "It's said he saved Wellington on the Peninsula through his wits."

"That's the only reason polite Society receives him. Remember that he also as good as murdered his young cousin there in order to get the title. He's nothing but a scoundrel."

Standish looked quickly around again. "Careful," he hissed. "I'd caution you not to forget the two duels."

"Have no fear that I will be fool enough to give him any reason to call me out. No, my besting of him will be far more subtle. And far more satisfying."

"Why do you care about the girl being ruined? I thought we were—"

Hammerton's lips were still curled in a semblance of a smile. "Because it suits my plan, dear cousin. Yes, it suits it very well indeed. Just leave the thinking to me."

"Good lord, Sebastian. Never expected to see you at such a gathering as this."

Lord Henry Ashton made his way to the corner of the ballroom where Branford stood. Whether by accident or design, there were few others near the tall figure of the earl, who was dressed entirely in black, save for the snowy white of his starched shirt and elegantly tied cravat. "Cecelia is an old friend of Lady Worthington, else wild horses couldn't drag me to such a sad crush." He raised an eyebrow in question as he beckoned a passing footman to bring them both a glass of champagne.

Branford gave his friend a brief smile, then continued to survey the crowd, eyes intent as a hawk hunting some unsuspecting prey. "I have my reasons, Henry."

Ashton snorted. "You sound as if you've stepped from some damned Radcliffe novel. It may make the ladies swoon—and don't give me that basilisk stare either. It may make most of your acquaintances quake in their boots but it has no such effect on me."

Branford chuckled and the hard planes of his face softened for a moment as his eyes lit with real humor. "I thank you for the set-down my friend, else I'd be in danger of becoming puffed up with the sense of my own consequence."

Ashton grinned. "Nonsense." He paused, his face becoming more serious. "Though I've never understood why you allow people to think you—"

Branford's face had hardened into its usual inscrutable mask. "Henry," he said, a note of warning in the tone.

"Damnation, Sebastian. I've become concerned about you of late. You're drinking far more than is good for you, not to speak of standing stud for half the wives of the *ton*. And you're neglecting Riverton, and I know how much you care—"

"Henry." The voice was even softer, but indicated it would brook no resistance. "You are a good friend. But even friends may go too far."

Ashton let out a sigh. "Very well," he muttered. "For now."

Branford swept the room with his gaze once more. "Do you know a Miss Chilton?" he asked abruptly.

Ashton looked puzzled. "Why yes, her aunt is a good friend of my mother's. But why do you ask?"

"Introduce me."

"Whatever for? Not your type at all."

"What do you mean?"

"Not a stunning young widow or a bored countess," answered Ashton frankly. "Not even terribly attractive. In fact, rather a bluestocking, half on the shelf. Lady Beckworth's her guardian. Family's come to town to give the pup of a brother some polish, so my mother says. They haven't got much blunt, though. Not likely either of them will be able to make much of a match."

Branford's eyes narrowed slightly at the news. "Nonetheless, introduce me."

His friend frowned slightly, then shrugged. "As you say, you must have your reasons. But I consider Lady Beckworth a friend of the family—though I know you well enough to know you wouldn't dream of toying with an innocent."

Ashton worked his way through the crowd to where a cluster of matrons sat gossiping among themselves while keeping an eagle eye on whom was dancing with whom. There was also a much younger lady at the edge of the group, her expression one that seemed to indicate her thoughts were anywhere but the ballroom.

"Miss Chilton." Lord Ashton bowed politely as the young lady started, her eyes betraying a brief flash of annoyance as she focused on the two gentlemen in front of her.

"Good evening . . . Lord Ashton." The tone was hardly welcoming.

"May I have the honor of presenting my friend the Earl of Branford."

"How do you do," she replied with a singular lack of enthusiasm as Branford bent over her hand in turn.

"May I have the pleasure of a dance, Miss Chilton?" he asked. The band was striking up a waltz. "Perhaps this one, if you are not taken." He had already noticed that the dance card dangling from her wrist was all but empty.

She seemed to hesitate for a moment, then rose slowly and placed her hand on his proferred arm. Ashton was right, he noted. She was no raving beauty. Her hair was merely brown, not a striking blond or glossy raven, and her mouth was a touch too wide, though obviously expressive. She was too tall and her curves not rounded enough for the tastes of most gentlemen. But her eyes, a hazel color flecked with green, had a depth that was intriguing, hinting at hidden facets not readily discernible on the surface.

However, if her aunt hoped to marry her off she had better employ another modiste, he noted. The dress was a disaster. The insipid mauve color clashed with her best features, her eyes, and the cut made her look gawky and ill proportioned. Girlish ruffles and bows were in abundance, and the effect was more appropriate for a female of twelve rather than twenty four. Branford, whose taste was acknowledged to be impeccable, nearly winced as he turned to face her full on.

She danced much better than he expected, moving with a lithe grace and matching his steps effortlessly. As he was deciding to forgo the usual compliments on her dress in favor of another less egregious social lie, she spoke first.

"As a matter of fact, I have been wanting to meet you, my lord."

Branford closed his eyes for an instant. Now would come the usual outrageous compliments or silly simperings that every unmarried girl felt obliged to offer up to a rich, titled bachelor. He had forgotten how much he loathed all of this. How had he allowed himself to be drawn into such a stupid, senseless bet? Ashton was right on another thing—he *had* been drinking too much.

Despite such thoughts, he replied in a neutral tone. "Is that so? And why is that, Miss Chilton?"

"Because in the paper you sent to the Botanical Society on the gardens at Riverton, you are mistaken in thinking that the purple flowers are *Scabiosa caucasica*. They do not grow in this climate. They are no doubt *Stokesia laevis*, which look very similar. Of course it is a reasonable error for someone unversed in botany to make."

It was not exactly what he expected to hear. He nearly trod on her foot. "What?"

"The flowers in the south garden. I take it you *are* the only Earl of Branford."

Branford stared at her, speechless.

"Mr. Simpson was too afraid to correct you, but I said that was utter nonsense—any sensible person would want to know of his error." She paused and regarded his stony face. "Oh dear," she sighed, half to herself. "I had looked forward to talking about the gardens with you, but it appears that, like most gentlemen, you disapprove of ladies who wish to have an intelligent conversation."

Branford recovered his wits. "No, Miss Chilton," he answered dryly. "On that I have formed no opinion, since I have little experience in having an intelligent conversation with a lady."

There was a pause. Alex smiled. "Touché, my lord."

In spite of himself Branford found himself smiling back. The girl had wit as well as backbone.

"You do not look half so dragonlike when you smile, you know. Or do you prefer to frighten people with that black scowl?"

Branford unconsciously drew his dark brows together.

"There, you see," she said. "You are doing it again. It is quite intimidating, you know."

"And you, Miss Chilton. Are you always so outrageous, or are you just hoping I will take you back to your chair so you can resume your own private thoughts and not have to be bothered with having to do the polite?" He watched a wave of surprise wash over her face. "You are not the only one capable of observing people," he added.

Her eyes met his for a moment, the green fleck alight with some emotion, before she dropped her gaze in some confusion.

"Now, about my gardens. What would you like—"

The music was drawing to an end and the surrounding couples were beginning to leave the floor. Branford found himself irritated that the dance was over so quickly. "It appears we will have to wait for another waltz. Shall we say the one after the supper break?"

"If you wish, my lord." Alex had composed herself and answered evenly, her chin thrust up slightly as if to say that she, at least, was not in the least bit intimidated by him.

"Good." He delivered her back to her aunt and it was only as he was walking away that he realized he had utterly forgotten the reason he had asked her to dance in the first place. He cursed under his breath. Now how had he been distracted? His purpose was to confirm the girl's availability and figure out a plan of seduction—and what had he done but begin a conversation on botany! Well, he had another dance. He would guide the conversation as he wished the next time around.

He took another glass of champagne and sought out an empty corner of the room. The look on his face was even more forbidding than usual, ensuring the solitude he desired. Something he couldn't quite put a finger on was bothering him and try as he might to shake the feeling, it kept drawing his attention to the half-obscured figure of Miss Chilton sitting silently among the turbaned matrons.

A lovely widow he had recently dallied with swept close by and tried to catch his eye, but he pointedly ignored her. He had no intention of dancing any more than he had to this evening. His booted foot began to tap impatiently on the polished parquet and once again he cursed his judgment—or lack of it—in letting himself become embroiled in such a situation.

Then it struck him. Miss Chilton had not once batted

her rather attractive lashes at him, nor had she simpered nor flattered him. On the contrary, he thought with a twitch of a smile. She had all but called him a gudgeon. There was something hidden in those interesting eyes of hers, but it was not artificial gaiety or a forced fawning. In short, she had not made any attempt to . . . flirt. The realization only served to increase his sense that something was not quite right about the whole thing. Surely if she was as experienced in the world as he had been led to believe . . .

A short, somewhat plump middle-aged gentleman had stopped to converse with Miss Chilton. Garbed in evening clothes that had most assuredly not seen Weston's hand, he looked as much a country dweller as the girl herself. But she was evidently glad to see him, as evidenced by the warm smile she bestowed upon him. Branford could make it out even through the swirling silks and flickering candles. She then rose and they began to make their way toward the supper room.

Branford moved through the crowd to where a sumptuous buffet had been laid out for the guests. Ignoring the platters of delicacies, he stopped quite near to where Miss Chilton and her acquaintance were seated enjoying a selection of succulent lobster patties. She appeared not to notice his arrival, not once turning her head or glancing his way. He made a point of moving two or three steps to his left, where he would be directly in her line of sight. Still not the slightest acknowledgment of his presence. Her attention was riveted on her companion who was speaking with great animation, punctuating his points with a flourish of his silver fork.

"Ah, there you are, Sebastian. Are you going to be so rag-mannered as to avoid me entirely tonight?"

Branford turned to face a petite blonde whose porcelain

skin and artfully arranged curls gave her the air of a china doll. He knew much better, however, than to be deceived by such an innocent appearance—few who knew her cared to match wills with Lady Ashton.

"Cecelia." He flashed one of his rare smiles as he bent over her hand. Thinking of his earlier statement to Miss Chilton, he mentally corrected himself. Lady Ashton was one of the few ladies who possessed great sense along with her more obvious charms. "I was merely waiting until the bevy of admirers thinned to a manageable number before storming their ranks."

"Fustian," she exclaimed, giving him a slight rap on the arm with her fan. "You, of all people, I wouldn't expect to toadeat me!"

Branford gave a low laugh. "Rarely have I been accused of being a toadeater."

"Of that I'm sure," she answered, a glint of amusement in her eyes. "Now, am I to be favored with a dance?" She consulted the card at her wrist. "I'm sure Henry will forgo the pleasure of the next waltz."

"I'm sorry. I'm promised for that one." His eyes strayed to Miss Chilton. Lady Ashton followed the subtle shift of his gaze and looked speculatively at him.

"Interesting," was all she said.

For the first time that he could remember, Branford felt a slight flush stealing over his face. Ashton saved him from having to make any reply by approaching them and slipping an arm around his wife's diminutive waist.

"I believe our dance is drawing nigh, my dear. It seems it is the only chance I shall have all evening of wresting you away from that damn group of jackanapes who insist on hovering around you."

"Mind your tongue, Henry," scolded Cecelia. "We are not at home."

"Wish we were. You know I abhor these tedious affairs," he grumbled.

"Then we shall leave as soon as you have done your duty with Lady Worthington." She smiled fondly at her husband before turning back to Branford. "And you, I have not excused you yet. I shall expect you to call on me in the next few days or I shall be extremely cross with you."

Branford gave an exaggerated bow. "Heaven forbid that I bring such a fate down on my head, madam. I shall present myself at Berkeley Square without fail."

He watched them depart arm in arm and felt a faint twinge at their obvious closeness. Then he turned on his heel, determined to get down to business.

Chapter Two

"How very interesting," remarked Lady Ashton softly as soon as they were some paces from Branford.

"What's that, my dear?"

"Sebastian and Alex Chilton."

"Don't be ridiculous! I don't know what he is up to, but a less likely pair I cannot imagine. You know Sebastian—probably just deucedly bored this evening and acting on some strange whim."

"Hmmph."

"Really, my dear. She is not at all the type of lady who would attract Branford."

"I am well aware she is not at all like the ladies he has been taking to bed, but—"

"Cecelia!" sputtered Ashton.

"Oh, Henry. Don't squeal like a stuck pig. Why on earth do you men think we know nothing about what goes on in the world?" She cast a mischievous look his way. "Why, I'm sure the gossip in the drawing rooms at tea is every bit as informative as it is at your club, and every bit as au courant."

Ashton had the grace to look discomfited.

"I have met Alex Chilton on several occasions," added Lady Ashton. "She is a most interesting young lady."

The music began.

"You must trust my judgment on this one. I have known

Sebastian for some time now, and if you think he has the least interest in a girl like Miss Chilton you have windmills in your head," said Lord Ashton as he slipped his arm around his wife, a touch more firmly than necessary.

"Oh? You don't think men find intelligent ladies attractive?"

Ashton looked warily at her. "Now, Cecelia, don't put words in my mouth. It's just that . . ." He knew he was trapped. Picking up the pace, he twirled her around and around to forestall any further conversation. Under his breath he muttered, "Not a chance."

Lady Ashton only smiled to herself.

Lord Branford had turned back and approached Miss Chilton. She was still engaged in an animated conversation with her friend and took no notice of his presence or the notes of the scale that announced the music was about to begin again. The gentleman, however, paled slightly and stammered something that caused her to stop in mid-sentence. She turned to look over her shoulder and it seemed to Branford that he saw a crease of irritation on her forehead.

"Is it really that time?" she asked. "Perhaps you could find another partner, my lord—I'm engaged in a most fascinating conversation with Mr. Simpson at the moment."

"No, Miss Chilton, I could not. I am sure Mr. Simpson will oblige you by waiting to continue his discourse until you return." He cocked a dark brow at the gentleman in question.

The man turned even paler and nodded vigorously. "Of course, of course. Miss Alexandra, I shall be more than happy to wait." He swallowed nervously.

Alex shot Branford a black look. "Very well."

As she began to rise she realized that her absorption in the conversation had caused her to neglect her manners. "Forgive me, but I have forgotten to introduce you."

Mr. Simpson's eyes widened and he looked as if he would have been well pleased if she had not noticed the omission. "I'm sure his lordship doesn't care to bother . . ." he mumbled.

"My lord, may I present Mr. Josiah Simpson."

The man shot to his feet and bowed low. Branford nodded.

"Mr. Simpson, this is the Earl of Branford. You remember. The one who is a bit confused about what grows in his gardens."

The poor fellow looked ready to expire on the spot. She turned to Branford. "Mr. Simpson is secretary of the Botanical Society. He is giving a very informative series of lectures on native English shrubs. Perhaps you would care to attend?"

Now the man was turning beet red and making choking sounds. Branford had to stifle a laugh. The chit was utterly outrageous, but not in any way he had been led to expect. Imagine, to challenge his intellect in so brazen a manner!

"Perhaps," he replied with an even tone. "But now, if you will excuse us, Mr. Simpson."

The man bowed once more, then sank into his chair in relief, using the large damask napkin to wipe the beads of sweat from his forehead. Branford took Alex's elbow in a firm grasp and guided her out to the dance floor. A slight buzz ran through the room. Eyes turned to see who it was that the Icy Earl chose to stand up with twice in one evening—and the only two dances he deigned to participate in at that.

Branford ignored the looks and concentrated on turning the conversation to his own purpose this time.

"Tell me, Miss Chilton, what do you do in town for amusement?" he asked before she had a chance to speak.

Alex looked at him blankly.

"Do you ride?" he persisted. It was considered quite fashionable for ladies of the *ton* to meet their admirers for a canter along Rotten Row during the afternoon hours. It would provide an excuse to spend more time with her.

"I enjoy riding in the country, but we do not keep much of a stable in town. It's too expensive. We just have a pair for my aunt's carriage and Justin—that is my younger brother—has his saddle horse, as of course a young man must."

An opening was there for him to take. He decided to cast subtlety to the wind and find out exactly where things stood. He lowered his dark lashes and spoke in a low mellifluous voice that rarely failed to get results.

"In that case, perhaps you will allow me to mount you."

Her face betrayed no understanding of what he had just implied. "I'm sure that is most kind of you, sir, but I could not possibly ask my aunt to incur the expense of stabling a mount solely for my own pleasure. She does enough as it is—" She stopped abruptly and bit her lip. "But of course that is no concern of yours. Forgive me for mentioning personal matters."

As she spoke, Branford felt a surge of anger.

The girl was a complete innocent in that regard. No lady the least interested in a dalliance could have failed to catch the innuendo of his last remark. Never had he sought to ruin a young girl! His sense of honor had always found the very idea repugnant and he felt nothing but contempt for men who found excitement in such a thing. His jaw tightened.

"Is something the matter, my lord?"

He brought his attention back to the moment. "What?"

"Your brows are drawn together in a most predatory manner. You look as if you are about to pounce on some poor creature."

"Someone shall feel my talons," he muttered under his

breath. Then he added, "My apologies, Miss Chilton. My thoughts were momentarily elsewhere."

She looked at him thoughtfully. "I can hardly blame you, sir. It's all so utterly boring, is it not?"

She had done it again. She had him smiling in spite of his dark mood. One thing was certain. A conversation with Miss Chilton was most certainly not boring.

Once again the music ended sooner than he expected. He escorted Alex back to a chair near her aunt but made no move to leave. "You seem to have a great knowledge of botany," he remarked.

Alex lifted her chin slightly. "I do, my lord." There was a glimmer in her eye that seemed to challenge him to ridicule her. "In fact, I am working on a book on native wildflowers and hope to have it published." It was obvious she expected him to turn on his heel or mouth some platitudes about the unsuitability of a young lady seeking to do such a thing.

"Indeed. What do you think of the work of Hopkins?"

He repressed a smile at the look of surprise on her face.

"You have read Hopkins?" she exclaimed.

"I have a modicum of education, Miss Chilton. Ignorance is one of the few things I have not been accused of."

She colored. "I did not mean to imply—"

"Of course you did," he interrupted. "You have been doing it all evening. Perhaps your opinions of the opposite sex are as fixed as those you choose to rail against." He knew he was being harsh, but he was curious as to how she would react to such a set-down.

Alex sat for a moment in silence. "Perhaps you are right, sir. I hadn't thought of it quite like that." She looked up to meet his gaze full on. "I shall endeavor not to act on preconceptions in the future. Now, do you truly care to know what I think of Mr. Hopkins or was that merely a ploy to set up your lecture?"

The girl had real spirit, he thought with grudging respect. Most men would have quailed at his cutting words. "I am most definitely interested in your thoughts, Miss Chilton."

She proceeded to elucidate on them in great detail, though through his own comments and questions, he revealed he was not a total neophyte.

"You are extremely knowledgeable, too, sir," she exclaimed, unaware of the pointed glances she and the earl were beginning to attract. "Do you keep specimen plantings at Riverton?"

"The gardens at Riverton are known for their variety—" He stopped abruptly, his mouth thinning into a grim line.

Did he imagine it, or did he see a flicker of sympathy cross her features?

"I have heard they are very beautiful," she said softly. "And they appear to be in good hands."

Damn the chit! How did she sense what a painful topic the Branford estate was to him?

"Yes, they are," he snapped, then quickly shifted the conversation to a less disturbing subject. "But as to specimen plantings, you have no doubt seen the latest arrivals from the East Indies at Kew Gardens?"

"Oh, I have heard they are marvelous." She gave a wistful sigh. "Aunt Aurelia's coachman has terrible rheumatism so I feel guilty asking her for the carriage. But my brother has promised he shall try to get his friend Baron Rutledge to drive me there, perhaps later this month."

"I believe I am free considerably sooner than that—say Thursday?"

Alex's eyes widened in surprise.

"I shall call for you at ten so you may have ample time to explore the grounds as well."

"Truly, sir? You would really drive me to Kew Gardens?"

"I am not in the habit of making idle promises, Miss Chilton. If I say I shall do something, you may count on it."

Her smile was radiant, transforming a merely pleasant face into one that was . . . captivating. "My lord, you are too kind!"

Few would have used such an adjective for him.

Then her face took on a look of concern. "I must admit, sir, I am still trying to learn all the rather silly rules which govern a lady's behavior in town so I do not embarrass my aunt or my brother. Is it permissible for me to drive out with you?"

"My tiger will accompany us and we shall travel in an open phaeton, so it is quite acceptable." He closed his eyes for an instant. How the deuce had he just engaged himself to spend the entire day with such a decidedly odd female?

"Thank you, my lord. I shall—"

Alex was interrupted by the arrival of her brother. Casting a dark look at Branford he reached for her hand. "Come, Alex. You are promised to me for this set." He nearly yanked her out of her chair in the haste to be off.

"Justin! Where are your manners? You would have Lord Branford think we were both brought up in a barn."

Justin's scowl deepened during the introductions and he barely made a civil bow before whisking his sister off to the dance floor.

Branford had no interest in remaining any longer at the ball. He turned and strode out of the room. He had matters to attend to at his club.

The man taking Branford's coat skittered away like a crab trying to avoid a crashing wave. The earl's face looked stormy indeed, and the manner in which he stalked through the rooms of the club left no doubt as to his mood. He stopped at where the betting book lay open and picked up the quill that lay next to it. Dipping it into the bottle of ink, he turned back a page or two, his brows drawn together as he scanned the entries. He paused momentarily, then with bold, angry strokes, slashed through the offending lines again and again until only an illegible black streak was visible. Throwing down the pen, he looked around the room.

"Wilton!"

The gentleman in question tightened the grip on his glass of brandy so that his knuckles were nearly white. A small group of his friends unconsciously took a step or two away from him.

With a few long strides Branford was beside him. "You and your friends were grossly mistaken as to the subject of our bet."

Wilton's mouth twitched spasmodically. "I—I never—"

"You will inform them that as of now, the wager has ceased to exist. If they have a problem with that, they may call on me."

"Of course, my lord." The relief was evident in Wilton's voice. "My—my apologies for any misunderstanding. I am sure . . ."

Branford made to go. "Oh, and one other thing." His tone was low but the fury in it was barely disguised. "I am not in the habit of blackening an innocent's reputation. If a whisper of this wager is ever breathed anywhere, I shall know where to look for satisfaction. I take it my meaning is quite clear. Be so kind as to inform the rest of your cronies."

Wilton swallowed and could only nod, not that Branford took any notice. He was already storming out of the room.

"I don't like it!" Justin jabbed at the bacon on his plate. "I won't allow a jaded rake to make sport with you."

Alex took a bite of her toast and continued reading the newspaper. "There is nothing to get so worked up about. I merely danced with the man."

"Twice!"

"And we had a conversation."

"A damned—excuse me, Aunt Aurelia—a deuced long one. Everyone was beginning to stare. What in heaven's name were you discussing for such an age?"

"Botany." She reached for the marmalade, suppressing a smile at the choking sounds coming from her brother's direction.

"Aunt Aurelia," he appealed. "Tell her she must not encourage Lord Branford's attentions. He's . . . dangerous."

Lady Beckworth poked her head up from behind a tome of Plato's works. "What was that, dear?"

Justin groaned.

"You needn't carry on so. I'm hardly a green girl just out of the schoolroom. And I'm hardly an attraction on the Marriage Mart, so there is no need to worry—"

"From what I have heard, there is cause to worry when Branford is around *any* lady. It's said he has no scruples at all. About anything! Why, most of the *ton* is terrified of him." Justin meant it as a warning but Alex only tossed her head.

"More fools they," she retorted. "I didn't find him in the least frightening. In fact, he is considerably more interesting than most of the gentlemen I've met so far. And he is quite well-read, you know."

Justin refused to give up. "You know what they say? That he as good as murdered his cousin to inherit the title. What say you to that? That's the kind of man he is. Not to speak of the men he's rumored to have killed in duels over . . . er . . ."

"Mistresses?" she suggested.

Justin was rendered speechless.

"Since you've always had the good sense to speak to me as if I had a brain in my head you must expect that I know as much as you and your male acquaintances do about the real world." Alex turned the page with a snap.

"What an idiot I am," he muttered, slashing at a pile of grilled kippers.

"Besides, you know as well as I how twisted rumors can be. Or have you forgotten the things that were said about Papa when we lived in Cornwall for a year? We had to leave when the talk got so bad. Imagine, the country folk getting in such a state, thinking he was a witch because he collected all manner of plants and roamed the countryside at all hours of the day."

Justin had the grace to color. He poked for a moment at the food left on his plate. "Nonetheless, the Icy Earl is a man to be avoided. Promise me that you will have no further conversation with him."

Alex folded the paper and put it aside. "You have given me no real reason to act in such a silly manner. Besides, it would be extremely difficult—unless you expect me to spend an entire day in silence. And it would hardly be polite, I might also add, seeing as he has kindly offered to drive me to Kew Gardens to see the newly arrived specimen plantings."

The fist came down with a thud that rattled the china. "Aunt Aurelia!" This time Justin was nearly shouting.

Aurelia laid her reading material on the table as well. "Are you two children having a spat?" she inquired over her spectacles.

Justin ran his hand through his hair. "Has no one in this family any sense but me? Surely you cannot condone Alex's association with a known rake and murder—"

Alex's quelling look cut off the last word.

Lady Beckworth surveyed the agitated faces of her niece and nephew. "Justin, Alex is more than of an age to decide for herself what acquaintances she wishes to make. A ride in an open carriage with a gentleman's tiger accompanying them is perfectly acceptable. And Lord Branford is received by even the highest sticklers of Society."

She paused. "But Alex, your brother's concerns are quite legitimate. You must admit you have little experience with the working of Society here in town. He is right to caution you to have a care. A reputation is not like a dress—once torn it is almost impossible to mend."

Both of them shifted uncomfortably in their chairs. Lady Beckworth picked up her book. "If you will excuse me, I am eager to finish a certain section of my translation before evening. And please don't forget we are promised to the Killington's rout tonight."

She gathered her things and left the breakfast room, leaving the two young people with much food for thought.

It was an even greater crush than the night before. Lady Killington's reputation as a splendid hostess ensured that her invitations would not be overlooked by those privileged enough to receive one. The sounds of violins and cellos floated through the immense ballroom, the flickering of hundreds of candles winked off the shimmering silks and jewels, creating a gallimaufry of color. Masses of exotic flowers added a special touch, their subtle fragrance wafting through the soft trill of laughter and animated conversation.

Alex tugged at a flounce on her sleeve to mask her discomfort. Why did she always feel so deucedly awkward at such evenings? Why couldn't she seem to master the art of dazzling smiles and fluttering eyelashes that other young ladies seemed to find so effortless? She sighed. It was simply no use. And why was she even thinking about it? Normally such frivolous thoughts about her demeanor or her appearance never even occurred to her. She sighed again. At least in such a crowd there should be a few members of the

Botanical Society present with whom to converse so the evening wouldn't be a complete waste.

"Miss Chilton."

There was no mistaking the rich baritone, though it was spoken quite softly. She turned to face a pair of glittering sapphire eyes.

"Good evening, my lord." She smiled, quite effortlessly because it was real. "Quite a crush tonight, is it not?"

Branford raised an eyebrow. "Come, Miss Chilton. You disappoint me. Surely you do not make a habit of uttering the usual polite platitudes." His face was deadpan, but there was a twinkle in his eyes.

"What would you prefer, sir? That I recite the phylum, genus, and species of that"— she glanced quickly around— "rare orchid over between the delphinium?"

"Which you no doubt know."

"Or perhaps you would prefer something more practical, as in if you move your right elbow a fraction of an inch you will send Lady Killington's no doubt priceless crystal vase to its demise."

Branford straightened with a start, narrowly averting disaster. How the devil hadn't he noticed the arrangement of flowers? He wasn't usually so clumsy.

Alex struggled without success to suppress a grin.

"Impudent chit," he murmured as he took her elbow and guided her to the dance floor.

"I should like to know more about your work, Miss Chilton. Tell me about the manuscript you are working on," said Branford as they began to move to the lilting melody. Once again, he couldn't help but notice how in tune she was with his movements, how she matched his steps with an effortless grace.

She looked up at him warily, as if searing his face for

some hint of mockery. He merely cocked his head expectantly but said nothing further.

"It is not a manuscript," she answered slowly. "Rather it is a series of watercolors on the wildflowers of Hampshire."

"You are an artist, then?"

She smiled at the thought. "Indeed not. I create no heroic scenes from history like Jacques Louis David, nor capture the likenesses of important people like Thomas Gainsborough. I merely record, as faithfully as I can, the nuance of detail and color in such everyday things as flowers. To me, the simple elements of the natural world have an inherent beauty as special as any face—" She stopped abruptly, as if afraid she had revealed too much of her feelings.

He didn't reply, but regarded her thoughtfully.

When the music had finished, Alex glanced around the crowded room. "Oh, I do so hope Mr. Simpson and Mr. Hepplewith are in attendance tonight. I wanted to ask them a question concerning a certain lily . . ." She trailed off as she continued to search the crowd.

Branford's height offered him a better vantage point. "I believe Mr. Simpson is over there." He guided her through the crush toward a large potted palm tree near the entrance to the card room. "He is with an elderly, rotund gentleman who appears to be wearing a rather outdated wig."

Alex smiled. "That is Mr. Hepplewith. He is quite interesting despite his odd appearance. I think you would like him, sir."

Before he could answer, she hurried ahead through the last few couples in the way. "Good evening, gentlemen. How nice to see you here. At least I shall be assured of some intelligent conversation for the evening."

Behind her, Branford cleared his throat.

"Oh!" Alex's hand flew to her mouth. "Of course, I didn't mean—"

Mr. Simpson stared wide-eyed, first at her, then at the earl, mesmerized as if waiting for a snake to strike its helpless victim.

Branford threw back his head and let out a hearty laugh. "I shall endeavor not to bore you excessively during the next waltz."

Alex managed a weak smile. "You are teasing me, Lord Branford."

"Which you richly deserve."

"Is this the author of the descriptions of Riverton, then?" inquired Mr. Hepplewith in a reedy voice. He exhibited none of the inhibitions of his colleague regarding the earl. "You have promise, young fellow. If you will apply yourself to the subject, we may make a botanist of you yet."

Alex's smile broadened. "Mr. Hepplewith is president of the Botanical Society. Mr. Hepplewith, this is indeed Lord Branford."

The two men bowed politely.

"Mr. Simpson you already know." Branford nodded in the man's direction, noting the fellow no longer jumped at his glance.

"Now, my lord. I have a question concerning the symmetry of the East gardens at Riverton," began Mr. Hepplewith. "Mr. Simpson is under the impression . . ." He paused to sample a lobster canape and take a glass of champagne from a passing footman.

"Alex!" A tall young man perhaps a few years older than she, approached. He was dressed fashionably enough, but the cut and material of his evening clothes clearly bespoke his lack of title or plump pockets. His face was not nearly so plain as his dress. He had well-cut, regular features and expressive brown eyes, now alight at the sight of his friend. The mouth, parted in a warm smile, was full, yet masculine, hinting at a strength of character, perhaps even stubbornness. Dark brown hair fell in curls that many a gentleman would have spent hours in front of the mirror to achieve.

"Hello, Charles."

Branford noted that he held the hand that Alex extended toward him a trifle longer than was necessary. He also noted that Alex's smile was quite radiant when she was truly happy to see someone. For some reason, he felt a flash of irritation which he quenched with a long swallow of champagne.

"A country set is forming. I pray that you will allow me the honor?" asked Charles Duckleigh.

"Will you excuse me." It was a statement rather than a question for she was already moving toward the center of the room with her partner.

Branford's lips compressed. Damn the chit, he thought, abandoning him to the Botanical Society—and just who was the pup to be on a first-name basis with her?

"Ah, as I was saying Lord Branford . . ."

The earl's manners made him stifle the urge to turn on his heel. But though he only intended to listen with half an ear, he found himself drawn into the conversation. It was novel to be spoken to as a fellow enthusiast rather than . . . murderer, or worse. Even Mr. Simpson seemed to lose the wary look on his face as he became animated in defense of his theory on how to arrange certain shrubs to ensure maximum bloom. And, in fact, the men were quite interesting.

As soon as Alex and her friend were out of earshot of the other men, Duckleigh leaned toward her. "Alex, I have heard rumors that *he* was bothering you . . ." His eyes strayed meaningfully in the direction of the earl's broad back.

"*He* is not *bothering* me in the least," she answered tartly.

The young man looked perplexed for a moment, then his face brightened. "Of course. You are much too smart to fall prey to his advances. Well, I am heartily glad to hear you have sent him about his business."

The steps of the dance took them apart for a bit. When they came together again, Alex adroitly changed the subject of discussion to the last lecture of the Botanical Society. That brought a light to Duckleigh's eyes and all mention of the Earl of Branford was forgotten.

When Alex returned, her face was slightly flushed from the exertion of the dance, a rosy glow that made her features appear alive and vibrant. Her eyes flashed with amusement at some remark Duckleigh had just whispered close to her ear.

Branford put down his glass and excused himself from the others. "I hope you are not too tired to grant me my waltz." He drew her hand onto his arm without waiting for a reply. "I believe the music is already starting."

Charles regarded him with narrowed eyes but stepped aside without a word.

Branford and Alex were also silent for the first few measures of the dance.

"Another member of your Society?" he asked abruptly.

"If you mean Charles, he is a cousin of Lord Halford and serves as his secretary. And yes, he is a member, an enthusiastic one. He is very interested in herbs."

"Among other things," said Branford under his breath. "Looks like a dull dog," he remarked out loud.

Alex cocked her head to one side. "To a man of your interests, perhaps."

"And just what do you mean by that?"

Alex looked at him unwaveringly. "It is well known that you are a true Corinthian, sir—an expert whip, a superb rider, and a deadly shot—"

"Have a care, Miss Chilton," he said softly. "Few men would dare to bait me thus."

Alex's eyes widened in surprise, then took on a look of acute embarrassment. "My lord"—she faltered—"I meant no—that is . . ." She let out a sigh. "Oh, it must be very unpleasant to be the subject of rumors and innuendo, is it not?"

It was Branford's turn to look surprised. It was not the response he had expected. But then again, he was quickly learning that with Miss Chilton one rarely knew what to expect.

"Just which of the rumors have you heard?"

"Well, there are the two duels."

"Ah yes, the duels. Pray, tell me how do they go at the moment?" There was an edge to his voice. "Do I simply put a period to some poor fellow's existence because I wish to continue dallying with his wife, or has it gotten more interesting? Perhaps he has actually found me between the sheets with his bride and demands immediate satisfaction," he said in a bitter tone. "Forgive me, Miss Chilton, if I shock you."

"Actually, as the story goes, it is the wife who demands satisfaction. Before she allows you to leave her bed to deal with the enraged husband."

Branford struggled to keep a straight face. "You should be spanked, young lady. How the devil do you have any notion of—"

"Because my brother credits me with enough sense to speak to me as he would to one of his male acquaintances."

"Then he should be spanked too."

"Yes, well, he actually implied that himself just this morning."

"For what reason?"

"I told him in no uncertain terms that I was perfectly capable of deciding who I may dance and converse with."

The humor immediately drained from Branford's face and Alex felt his arm stiffen around her waist. There was a perceptible pause before he spoke again. "What else have you heard?"

"Everything, I imagine." She met his gaze squarely and there was no question that he saw a welling of sympathy in the depths of her eyes.

"Then you are either very brave or very foolish," he said coldly.

Alex frowned. "I think I am neither, sir."

Damn the chit. She was truly keeping him off balance and it was a strange feeling.

"Give you no countenance to rumors?"

She didn't answer for a moment. "Growing up, I would hear things that were . . . twisted versions of the truth. My father was the subject of much speculation due to his inquiries into the natural world. In Cornwall he was rumored to have been a witch due to his nocturnal ramblings and collecting of odd plants and specimens. Needless to say, we were soon forced to leave the area. So I prefer to judge for myself."

A ghost of a smile reappeared on Branford's face. "The scientist in you, Miss Chilton. Empirical knowledge only." He steered her back toward the potted palm. "I believe your Society eagerly awaits your return—a safe haven. I hope I have not reneged on my promise not to bore you." He bowed slightly. "Good evening."

"My lord . . ."

But he had already turned and disappeared in the crowd.

Branford wandered through the card room and helped himself to a glass of brandy. He needed something stronger than champagne to ease the knot deep inside. He swore to himself as he threw back the last of the spirits. Usually he had his emotions under tight rein. What has happened tonight to cause him to feel so on edge? It was disconcerting to be so—"

"My lord. I would like to have a word with you, if you please."

The voice was at his shoulder, trying hard to sound both deep and self-assured.

The earl turned to face a young man not quite his own height. The face was only vaguely familiar but the flashing color and intensity of the eyes were all too recognizable.

"Who the devil are you?" muttered Branford, though he knew full well what the answer was going to be.

"We were introduced last night. I am Justin Chilton, sir. Miss Alexandra Chilton's brother. I wish to have a word with you." He nodded toward the hallway. "The library is empty."

When the door was firmly closed, Justin took a deep breath, his chin coming up in precisely the same manner as his sister's when she felt challenged.

"Sir, I must ask you to refrain from dancing with my sister again. In fact, I would prefer that you refrain from any further contact whatsoever."

Branford regarded him with an icy stare that usually set men to quaking in their boots. The young man's jaw clenched, but he refused to blink.

"Your sister is of an age to make her own decisions. She knows what she is about."

"She does *not* know what she is about here in town. She knows her books and her plants, and her eccentric friends at the Botanical Society, not the rules and the . . . the games that Society and the *ton* likes to amuse themselves with. Therefore I must insist that you cease your attentions."

The earl's voice dropped to nearly a whisper. "Just what are you implying, Mr. Chilton?"

Justin took a deep breath, his brows knitted together. "I have very little experience in this sort of thing," he said honestly. "No doubt I shall say it badly." He took another breath. "I mean no disrespect to you, sir. How you choose to . . . conduct your affairs is not for me to comment on. It is my sister I am concerned about. Despite her age and her ideas on the world she has very little experience with . . . well, the opposite sex. I do not wish to see her hurt. I thought that if I spoke to you, man to man, you might agree to seek . . . what you wish with someone who understands how things are done here."

It was well said. Normally he would have ignored such a pup or sent him slinking away with a scathing set-down. But there was something about his quiet determination, the set of his shoulders, the earnest concern for his family that reminded Branford of another young man . . . The earl's lips compressed.

"Are you a good shot, Chilton?"

A muscle in Justin's jaw twitched but his chin rose even a fraction higher. "I am considered adequate among my acquaintances at home."

"I don't believe I've seen you at Manton's."

Justin colored. "I do not have either the funds or the connections to gain entrance there yet."

Branford sighed and reached into his coat pocket. He thrust a thick, engraved card into Justin's hand. "Tell Watters I sent you. He will arrange for everything."

Justin looked utterly confused. "I—I don't understand. You are standing me for Manton's?" His face slowly took on a dark look. "I cannot be fobbed off that easily, sir. I will not abandon my sister just to gain entrance to the most exclusive—"

"I have a proposal to make," cut in Branford.

Justin fell silent, a frown still clouded his features.

"I prefer not to have to deal with your histrionics every time I choose to converse with your sister—I commend you for at least having the sense to do it in private this time. But any more such efforts to guard your sister will only be damaging to her reputation if they become public knowledge, not mine. And they most certainly will become extremely tiresome to me, for I should be forced to deal with you."

He paused. "I have no intention of hurting your sister, Chilton. I give you my word on that. If you ever feel I have not lived up to it, I shall meet you on whatever terms you care to offer."

"Then why do you set me up at Manton's?"

"Because I am an excellent shot, Chilton. If we meet, I prefer that you be *more* than adequate—contrary to what you hear, I take no pleasure in murdering boys."

Justin studied the hard, impenetrable face before him. "Very well, sir," he said slowly. "I will accept your word as a gentleman."

"Good. Now kindly stay out of my sight!"

Branford stalked from the room and retrieved his greatcoat from a footman. As he stepped into the cool night air, he shook his head ruefully.

Driving a bluestocking, on-the-shelf young lady to Kew Gardens for a day of looking at plants.

Sponsoring a green pup to Manton's.

If he didn't have a care, it would be his *own* reputation among the *ton* that would soon be in shreds.

Chapter Three

"I hadn't imagined the leaves of *Colocasia esculenta* were so green," murmured Alex. "I mean such a rich green, rather more viridian than emerald, but much deeper than apple . . ." Her voice trailed off as she stared into the distance. It was another quarter mile before a bump in the road jarred her from her reverie.

"Oh dear, my lord, I fear I have been frightfully rude, haven't I? Why, I haven't said a word to you in ages!"

Branford smiled as he guided his grays around a mail coach with consummate skill. "Not at all, Miss Chilton. I commend you for not acting like a miss newly out of the schoolroom who feels she must prattle away regardless of having anything worthwhile to say."

Alex laughed. "I'm afraid I'm usually prattling on about something, though as for acting like a schoolroom miss, I doubt that's possible at my age."

"On the shelf, are you?" he inquired, cocking one eyebrow.

There was an almost imperceptible pause before she answered. "Yes, thank goodness, and well glad of it."

He slanted a sideways glance at her rigid features, his curiosity piqued by her response. But before he could say anything more, she sighed and spoke again. "There was so much to take in!"

He let himself be distracted. "You enjoyed yourself?"

"Oh, my lord, it was truly wonderful. Everything was so lush and vibrant—and the color! I cannot thank you enough." She smiled at him. He knew many ladies who would kill to look as radiant and sincere as Alex did at that moment.

"My pleasure." And to his surprise, he found that he meant it.

A comfortable silence reigned once more as Alex seemed lost once more in thoughts on the gardens and Branford remained intrigued by her reaction regarding being on the shelf. Why, he had always thought it ridiculous that young girls were meant to marry before they had a chance to become interesting, but somehow he didn't think that was what Miss Chilton meant. He wondered exactly what she did mean.

"My lord . . ." Alex spoke softly, barely audible above the clatter of the phaeton's wheels.

Branford was roused from his thoughts and turned his head expectantly.

"I was wondering if I might ask a favor of you. That is, another one, since I regard your driving me to Kew Gardens as a rather large one as well, but . . ." She faltered.

Branford's eyebrows shot up. "'Tis the first time I've seen you at a loss for words, Miss Chilton. Come now, don't you females practice this sort of thing? It certainly seems most of you have it down to a fine art. I do believe, however, that you are supposed to lower your lashes demurely and flutter them a few times when making the request."

Alex stiffened and her face colored. "Forgive me, sir. You are right to ridicule me. I am well aware I have no feminine charms. And I have no right to ask—"

"It wasn't meant as ridicule, Miss Chilton. I was merely teasing you."

Her eyes remained locked on the road ahead. The silence was now filled with tension. Branford swore to himself. She was difficult to figure out. He pulled the horses to an easy walk so he could turn his full attention to her.

"Miss Chilton, I apologize if I have offended you. Now please continue and ask me what you intended."

"It is of no import."

"Don't be a peagoose."

"I am not acting like—" She stopped. "I am, aren't I. I'm sorry." Her chin came up as she turned to face him. "I have little practice in asking a gentleman—or anyone for that matter—for his aid. You embarrassed me."

"It was badly done of me." Lord, she had as much damnable pride as a man! "It is I who am sorry."

Alex took a deep breath. "What I was wondering is, well, during the Peninsula campaign, you were credited for saving Wellington from ambush?" It was phrased as a question.

He nodded.

"You deciphered a code?"

He nodded again, intrigued as to where things were headed. Certainly in no direction he had ever explored with a female before.

"Are you an expert in cryptology?"

Would Miss Chilton never cease to surprise him? "I am fairly conversant with the principles from my work in the army."

"Well, I have been struggling for an age but I can't make heads or tails of it—I seem to have no aptitude for the principles of logic underlying cryptology, and I can't find a decent book on the subject—"

"I take it, Miss Chilton, you have a code you wish to decipher?"

It was Alex's turn to nod.

"And just how did you come by it?"

"It was tucked into one of my father's books, one of the ones he had with him the night he was driving home and had his accident." A puzzled look passed over her face. "He had never written in such a manner before. It is the oddest piece of paper. The letters are jumbled together in the most nonsensical way, and there are little symbols that look like axes or some such things . . ."

"Would you like me to take a look at it?"

Alex let out a rush of air. "Oh, if it wouldn't be too much trouble. I keep thinking, it must mean something important. Father was not one to do anything . . . frivolous or whimsical. It is as if he were trying to . . . hide something, or tell us something important that he wished no one else to see."

Branford could not help noticing that the straightforward appeal in her eyes was infinitely more persuasive than any fluttering of eyelashes or coy looks—she was quite wrong about not having any charms. "Perhaps you might show it to me when we arrive at your aunt's."

She flashed a grateful smile, then turned her gaze back to the road, again seemingly lost in thought. But this time the silence didn't last nearly as long.

"You sold out your commission and returned home from the war when you . . . inherited the title?"

His hands tightened on the reins. He nodded stiffly.

"It must have been a very difficult time for you." She stole a glance at his stony features. "How was your cousin killed?"

He nearly caused the grays to break stride with a cow-handed jerk on the reins. No one had ever asked about it, except Henry and Cecelia.

"I'm sorry. If you would rather not . . ." she said softly.

To his own surprise, he found himself answering. "My young cousin Jeremy had insisted on serving in my regiment. I had spent quite a lot of time at Riverton after the death of my parents, and being some years older, I think he—we got on very well together. Neither of us had siblings." His voice became softer. "He was . . . a good lad." He couldn't quite believe he was actually talking about this. Yet somehow he kept going. "We were deployed against a much larger Spanish force. They had an artillery detachment dug in on a hill above our forces. It was wreaking havoc with our troops. I was ordered to attack with my cavalry and take it out. Needless to say, it was an extremely dangerous assignment." He paused, his jaw tightening at the memory. "I tried to send Jeremy back to headquarters as a courier. He wouldn't hear of it. I—I could have ordered him, but he would never have forgiven me. Perhaps that doesn't make sense to you but—"

Alex instinctively reached out a hand and touched his for the briefest moment before withdrawing again. "I believe I understand exactly what you mean, sir."

His voice now had a raw edge to it. "The charge was successful, but the cost to my men was enormous. When I found Jeremy under the tangle of mangled horses and shattered bodies he was still alive. But there was nothing I could do. His wounds were too bad. He died in my arms."

She didn't speak for the longest time.

He was both surprised and grateful. How was it she seemed to have the knack for doing the right thing?

She finally broke the silence. "You must miss him very much."

"I miss him terribly."

Nothing else was said for the rest of the ride home.

Alex sensed something was amiss. The first knock on her aunt's door went unanswered, and when the manservant finally made his way down the hall and flung it open, she could see from the expression on his lined face that all was not well.

"What is it, Givens? Is Aunt . . ." she cried.

"It's Mr. Justin, Miss Alex. He's had a bad fall from his horse. The doctor is with him now."

She hastily undid her bonnet and pelisse and let them drop to the floor in a heap. Branford had entered behind her.

"How did it occur?" he inquired.

"The young gentlemen were engaging in some races in the park. Apparently Mr. Justin's saddle came undone. Mr. Hartley and another friend brought him home not half an hour ago. He was unconscious, Miss Alex, and white as a sheet."

Alex gave a little cry. "I must go to him!" She turned to Branford. "Please. Excuse me."

"Of course. The other matter will certainly keep until another time."

He resettled the curly brimmed beaver hat on his head and walked down the steps of the town house to where his tiger was walking the grays up and down the street. But instead of mounting the phaeton, he paused for a moment, then walked back to the mews. A young groom was rubbing down a stocky, aging chestnut gelding. Branford's appraising eye quickly noted it was an ordinary animal at best, with neither great fleetness nor great stamina.

"Is this Mr. Chilton's mount?"

The boy nodded. "Aye, sir. The one wot's had the accident."

"Where is the tack?"

A jerk of the head indicated one of the stalls, where a worn saddle hung over the door. The Chiltons, noted the earl as he ran his hand lightly over the leather, were definitely not plump in the pocket. Though well cared for, the saddle was old. It was no wonder it had broken. Nonetheless, his fingers ran down the girth, then stopped abruptly. There were no signs of fraying where it had come apart. The ends were smooth and clean, right down to the last half inch, which had been left to snap on its own. There was no question that it had been cut with a sharp instrument.

Justin winced as Alex straightened the pillow. "Still aches like the devil," he muttered, fingering the egg-shaped swelling on the back of his head.

"It's lucky you have a thick skull," she answered with a smile, though a chill knifed through her every time she thought about how things might have turned out. It was a miracle he had suffered no more serious injury than a knock on the head. "And it must be even thicker than I would have imagined, to try to race Artemis. Why, the poor old thing must have stumbled and sent you over his ears."

Justin flushed slightly. "He may be no primer goer but a gentleman can't back off from sport with his friends even if his mount is a nag sure to be beaten."

It was clear that more than his head was bruised. "Of course not," she said quietly. "Perhaps you might pay a visit to Tattersall's and choose a more suitable animal."

"We can't afford it." There was no bitterness in his voice, merely practicality and maybe a touch of longing.

"We've managed quite well. Town has not been quite as expensive as Aunt Aurelia and I had thought. I think we can manage the extra expenditure."

He frowned. "You should have a new gown, then. Something more, I don't know—dashing."

Alex looked away. "We're hardly going to waste money on me," she muttered, trying to push away her own sudden longing. Why in heaven's name should she care about looking well? There was no earthly reason not to be content with the gowns she had, even if they were outdated and not terribly flattering.

She quickly changed the subject. "The doctor thinks you need only stay in bed another day or two."

"A day or two!" he protested. "I feel quite well enough right now." He made as if to rise, then fell back with a sharp intake of breath.

Alex said nothing, but went to the window to rearrange the curtains in such a manner as to shield the bed from the late afternoon sun.

The door opened and the maid brought in a large tray of tea things and a plate of fragrant cakes fresh from the oven. Lady Beckworth followed.

"I thought we might take tea with you, Justin, now that you are feeling more the thing. I'm glad to see you have some color back—you had us quite worried, you know."

"Sorry." He slanted a glance at his sister. "But as Alex has said, we're both too hardheaded to come to any harm."

Lady Beckworth seated herself and began to pour. "Let us hope that no more accidents happen." She turned to Alex. "I just realized, my dear, that I have totally forgotten to ask you how your visit to Kew Gardens was. I know how much you were looking forward to it."

"It was more than I ever dreamed. The plants . . . oh, how can I describe it!" She sighed. Then noting Justin's scowl, she added. "And as you can see, I have arrived safely home with my virtue intact, I assure you."

"It's not a joking matter," said Justin, glowering.

Lady Beckworth continued as if unaware of the interchange between the two young people. "I hope Lord Branford did not take offense at things seeming to be at such sixes and sevens in the house."

"Of course not. He was quite aware of what had happened."

"You asked him in?" Justin's voice rose slightly.

"I wished to consult with him on something."

"What possible—" began Justin. "No." His eyes closed briefly as he put two and two together. "You didn't ask him about that damned—sorry, Aunt Aurelia—deuced letter!"

Alex's chin shot up. "It's none of your concern."

Justin groaned. "For heaven's sake, Alex. You know Father was in his own world at times, especially at that time. It's nothing but a manifestation of that." He threw up his hands. "It's no doubt nothing more than his own private rantings. Let it go. It's not important."

"Then why should you care what I choose to do?"

"Because I don't wish to see you made a laughingstock of the town. Secret codes indeed! Why, the *ton* will think we are odder than they already do!" exploded Justin.

"I'm sorry we embarrass you," she said quietly.

"Alex! I didn't mean that. I meant—"

"And I hardly think Lord Branford is one to engage in idle gossip." She rose stiffly. "If you will excuse me, I have some work I would like to finish while the light is still good enough."

Justin watched her go with a stricken face, feeling helpless in so many ways.

"I trust your brother is on the mend?"

Alex gave a start at the low baritone voice, then turned with a smile from watching the country dance in progress.

"The doctor finally allowed him out of bed this afternoon. I'm not sure who was more pleased—Justin or myself. I admit I should have been loath to have to listen to his rantings and complaints of boredom for another day."

Branford smiled. "Youth has little patience. Or little sense."

Alex looked at him with a mischievous expression. "Were you never young, sir?"

His mouth twitched. "I can't remember."

She laughed lightly, her eyes twinkling with humor. The thought occurred to him that in anyone else it would have been broadly flirtatious. "And just how old are you?"

"Thirty-three."

"Good Lord. Ancient!"

He took her arm and guided her to a less crowded part of the room. Then he fetched something to drink, a glass of ratafia punch for her, champagne for himself.

"Here is to good health from now on in the Chilton household."

Alex's face clouded for a second. "Yes," she agreed. "Yes. To no more . . . accidents."

Branford eyed her curiously, but let the question on his lips die. Instead he spoke of another matter. "I have been meaning to ask you if you would still like me to take a look at the piece of paper you found in your father's books?"

"Oh." She was pleased he had not forgotten. "If it is not too much trouble—"

"Miss Chilton," he interrupted. "I have come to expect a more rational conversation with you than with most young ladies. Please do not simper or prevaricate with me. I would not offer if indeed it was too much trouble. I assure you, I am not in the habit of doing things I do not wish to do."

"Yes. I would."

"Very well. Shall I call tomorrow at say, eleven?"

"That would be fine."

"Good. Now that we have settled business matters, perhaps we might enjoy a dance."

He placed his hand on her forearm. His touch was surprisingly light, but for the first time she was aware of the strength in the long, graceful fingers. She found herself enjoying the sensation of them on her bare skin. In fact they sent a tiny shiver up her arm.

"Are you cold?"

"No, not at all," she replied, hoping he didn't notice the faint blush on her cheeks.

The music began.

She wasn't even sure what they conversed about. Somehow, her concentration seemed to wander. Indeed, she might have been speaking gibberish for all that she was aware of the words coming out of her mouth. The only things that made any impact on her senses were odd—the presence of his hand at the small of her back, the movement of his muscled thighs close to the rustling folds of her dress, the scent of bay rum and something she couldn't name.

She was vaguely aware of the notes ending, of couples leaving the dance floor, of being guided across the room to where her friends were arguing over a monograph on ferns. Before she could roust herself from the strange mood that had overtaken her, he was gone.

He must think her a bloody idiot, she told herself, the earlier blush coming back in full force. Her eyes closed in acute embarrassment. How could she possibly behave in such a—

"Alex!"

Her eyes flew open.

"I have been looking all over for you," said Charles Duckleigh rather pointedly. However his ill humor could not hold up in the face of his obvious excitement over some matter. "My cousin has graciously arranged for the Duke of Wrexham to invite members of our Society to view his collection of rare orchids! And he has even offered me use of his carriage for the occasion. Mr. Simpson and Mr. Hepplewith suggest that we go on Wednesday next."

"Oh, how very nice." It was strange. She seemed to have no trouble focusing on things now.

"My I have the honor of escorting you on the trip? We shall bring a picnic to enjoy on the grounds and be back by suppertime."

"I shall be delighted," she replied, noting the look of rapture on his face. "How very influential you are becoming," she added with a playful smile.

It was said lightly, but Duckleigh couldn't help but throw back his shoulders a fraction, causing his chest to puff out.

Oh dear, she thought, the smile still on her lips. Young men could be so very silly at times.

"Lord Branford is here to see you, Miss Alex."

"Oh, do show him in, Givens." Alex unconsciously smoothed the skirt of her sprigged muslin dress as she rose from the sofa in the small parlor.

"Good morning, Miss Chilton."

The earl looked as if he had come from riding. He was dressed in snug-fitting breeches, which showed off the solid muscularity of his thighs, and polished Hessians. A finely tailored riding coat of claret melton fitted his broad shoulders with nary a wrinkle. His long, dark hair was slightly ruffled by the wind, softening the chiseled planes of his face.

Good heavens, thought Alex with a start, the gossips

were certainly right on one thing—he was devilishly good-looking. She pushed such notions quickly aside. "Good morning, my lord. If you'll follow me to the library, please." She hoped she sounded businesslike. For some reason, her voice felt as if it were catching in her throat.

He gestured for her to lead the way.

She pushed open the heavy oak door. "Forgive the disarray," she said, throwing a rueful look at the massive table covered with papers and piles of books, some opened, some stacked one on top of the other. "I fear both my aunt and I are engaged in projects at the moment that occupy all . . . our attention," she finished lamely. She hadn't realized things looked quite so chaotic.

Branford smiled in understanding. "Neatness is, no doubt, the work of idle hands," he remarked as he walked toward a small easel set by tall leaded glass windows that faced north.

"Really my lord, I'd rather you didn't—"

It was too late.

He had already moved around to observe the work in progress. For what seemed like an age he stared at it, not saying a word.

"It's not nearly finished," she finally stammered. "Truly, it's not meant to be seen by anyone yet . . ."

He looked up at her words. "It's the hibiscus from Jamaica. The one you admired at Kew Gardens."

She nodded.

"You are doing it from memory?"

She nodded again. "I find I have a good eye for color and detail, though I wish I could do it from life." A guilty look stole across her face. "I did, however, steal a tiny petal and put it in my reticle."

"It is exquisite." The look that appeared momentarily in his eyes sent a burst of unaccustomed warmth shooting through her. "Do you have some of your other paintings here? I should very much like to see them."

Alex looked as if to say something, then moved to the table. She cleared a book off of a leather portfolio and untied the silk ribbons. "Some of these are not yet finished either," she began.

He took the portfolio from her hands and carefully opened it. One by one he studied the delicate watercolors, spending what seemed to her an inordinate amount of time on each one.

"You are prodigiously talented, Miss Chilton."

Alex felt herself blushing like a schoolgirl.

He retied the ribbons and handed the portfolio back to her. The usual inscrutable look was back on his features.

He cleared his throat. "You have the piece of paper here?"

"Yes." She went around to the other side of the table and began fumbling through a pile of books. "I made a copy of it, in case you would like to take it with you."

"I should like to see the original too, of course."

"Of course."

She finally found what she was looking for and handed him a single sheet of foolscap, dog-eared and heavily creased. He unfolded it and stood, head bent, studying its contents.

"Hmmph."

"Yes?" she asked expectantly.

He was silent for a few more minutes. There was another "Hmmph" and then he looked up.

"Well?"

"It follows none of the more basic patterns that come readily to mind. I shall need to spend more time on it."

She hid her disappointment. "It's probably of no matter anyway," she sighed. "As Justin keeps saying, it's most likely just a list of new plants and where he found them—he could be extremely secretive at times, and the use of code was perhaps just another manifestation of that. There is really no urgency to it, sir."

Branford didn't answer but compared her copy with the original. Satisfied, he tucked her version into his pocket. "Your brother, I take it, is suffering no ill effects from his accident?"

A troubled look came to her face at the mention of the last word. "No, he is quite fine, thank you."

Still, the look of worry remained.

"Is something troubling you, Miss Chilton?"

She regarded him with a slightly defiant air. "You will no doubt think me a foolish female—Justin does."

"I shall think you foolish only if your pride prevents you from speaking out on something that is obviously causing you concern. It is not a weakness to seek advice, you know."

Alex hesitated, then let out a little sigh. "Very well. I am disturbed by the number of accidents that have befallen my brother in the last three months."

Branford's eyebrow shot up. "This was not the first?"

She shook her head. "A small bridge collapsed at Aunt Aurelia's estate early one morning when Justin was out riding. Once again, it was only by the purest of luck that he was not seriously injured—or worse." She shuddered slightly at the memory.

"Was he the only one who rode regularly at that hour?"

Unconsciously, Alex knitted her hands together. "Yes. And then, just a short time later while on his way to Oxford with his good friend Frederick Hartley, the wheel came off Mr. Hartley's carriage. The coachman broke his leg in the mishap."

"There is a plausible explanation for all these things. Accidents do occur, Miss Chilton."

"Yes, I know. But the coincidence is troubling, to say the least." Again she paused. "I looked at Justin's saddle. You may think me melodramatic, my lord, but the girth looked tampered with. The break was too clean, as if it were . . . cut."

So she had noticed. Her eye for detail certainly saw well beyond her palette.

His face became very serious. One hand came up to rub along his jaw. "Why do you think anyone would wish to harm your brother?"

Her hand flew up in exasperation. "That is what makes no sense. I can think of no earthly reason! It certainly isn't for money or title—oh!" She broke off, her face tight with embarrassment.

Branford gave a little smile. "Do go on, Miss Chilton."

"He has no enemies, does not run with a fast crowd, gamble or—"

"Bed other men's wives?" suggested the earl.

"I should think it highly unlikely," she answered, coloring slightly at the earl's subtle self-mockery. "He is quite attached to a Miss Anne Lockwood, a childhood friend, and hopes to pay his addresses to her. So, apparently, does a baronet from Sussex. But she is a sweet, biddable girl fresh from the schoolroom. Her father is quite well off, but no Croesus. His title is minor—she is hardly one to inspire murder."

Branford could not suppress another smile. "Hardly," he agreed.

"So you think me an hysterical female?" There was a note of challenge in her voice.

"I think you are quite observant. And I tend to agree with you that the coincidences seem rather forced."

A look of relief flooded her face. "At least *you* don't think me mad. Well, I intend to get to the bottom of it."

Branford's smile disappeared. "Just what do you mean?"

"Naturally I intend to find out who is responsible, and why."

"And just how do you intend to do that?"

Her chin shot up. "I plan to investigate the matter thoroughly. I don't intend to stand aside and let someone kill my brother, sir!"

"I suggest you stick with your painting, Miss Chilton. Let your brother deal with the matter."

A spark of anger flashed through her. "And stick with embroidery and tatting and the pianoforte as well, no doubt. Of course a *female* couldn't possibly set her mind to something serious."

"Don't be bacon brained. That is not what I meant—"

"Ah, thank you, Lord Branford! At least you acknowledge that I *have* a brain," she said acidly.

"What I meant," continued Branford in exasperation, "was it is a dangerous course you are setting—"

"Thank you for your advice, my lord, but there is no need to concern yourself in my affairs. It is a family matter. And I believe we have finished our other topic of business, so good day to you."

The earl could hardly believe his ears. The chit was dismissing him! His eyes narrowed. "I think not, Miss Chilton. Finished our business, that is. For if it is business, then surely you are aware that payment must be made for services rendered."

Alex looked startled, then quickly recovered herself. "You must name your price now, sir, so that I know whether I can afford it."

His eyes glanced toward the window. "The hibiscus."

"My painting!" she cried. "My paintings are not for sale."

He removed the folded paper from his pocket. "No doubt you are already regretting having admitted that you cannot solve every conundrum in the universe." He dangled it in front of her nose. "I'm sure you will eventually figure it out."

Alex flushed, whether in anger or dismay was impossible to tell.

"All right," she said in a voice barely louder than a whisper.

"What was that?"

"I agree to your terms, my lord," she replied. "You may have the painting when you have deciphered the letter."

The slight smile returned to his lips. "You drive a hard bargain, Miss Chilton, but we have a deal. Good day."

"Wretch!" she muttered as his tall, elegant figure sauntered out through the door.

Lord Ashton ran his hand down the hock of the big gray, then turned to observe the perfectly matched horse tied alongside. "What think you, Sebastian?"

Branford ran his critical eye over both animals. "A little narrow in the chest, but not a bad pair for the price."

At this, the dealer let out his breath. "A very fair price, if I say so myself, your lordship. But of course, for any friend of yours—"

A quelling look from the earl silenced the man.

Ashton straightened. "Appreciate the help. Lord knows, you have the best eye for horseflesh of anyone."

"Happy to be of assistance, Henry. Are these all you wish to purchase today?"

His friend nodded. "Doing any business yourself?"

"No, but if you are finished, I shall have a look around.

Thought I'd take a look at the chestnut hunter Bagley was raving about. Hear he's up for sale today."

Ashton waved him on. "Go ahead. I'll settle up here. And don't forget Cecelia expects you to call on her this afternoon."

"I will do so without fail."

Branford strolled off. Sale day at Tattersall's was always interesting. He watched an acquaintance from White's, a foppishly dressed, haughty second son of a duke, haggling over a colt and suppressed a grin. The animal was showy, but spindleshanked and would no doubt turn out to be a weak mount with a miserable gait. And the price was nothing short of a fleecing.

He turned away, but had only gone a short distance before he noticed another deal being discussed. Despite himself, he paused.

Justin Chilton was examining the teeth of a bay stallion with obvious inexperience.

"Not more than five years old, sir. A solid horse, and runs like the wind."

More like twelve and a plodder, thought Branford, who couldn't help but overhear the conversation.

"I don't know," said Justin uncertainly. "He seems a little skittish to me, and the price—"

"It's a very good price, sir. You'll do no better, I assure you."

What concern was it of his? the earl told himself. The pup had no business coming to a place like Tattersall's without someone to show him the ropes. He'd learn a good lesson by being fleeced. Still, something kept him from walking away and leaving the young man on his own. Damnation, from the back, he looked just like his cousin, even had the same way of holding his head when deep in thought . . .

Justin reached out to stroke the bay's head, but the animal shied away with a snort.

"Spirited stallion, he is—" began the dealer.

"Unstable is more the word."

Branford's low voice interrupted the man, who whirled around, an angry retort on his lips until he saw who had spoken.

"Lord Branford!" The man rubbed his hands together nervously. "The young gentleman didn't tell me he was a friend of yours. Of course there are other mounts I could show him."

Justin bowed a civil greeting to Branford. Yet despite a resolve to maintain his disapproval of the earl, he was not unaware of the man's reputation as a supreme connoisseur of horseflesh. He found himself blurting out, "So you would not recommend the animal, sir?"

"Indeed, I would not. A waste of your blunt."

Justin stared wistfully at some of the other fine stallions. "I'm afraid he's really the only one I can afford—and even then, it's more than I should spend. I was hoping to have something left over for a new gown for my sis—" He stopped abruptly, acutely embarrassed for having spoken so familiarly about personal matters, especially to someone he had determined to treat with coolness.

Branford found himself liking the lad for his honesty. He liked him even more for his concern for his sister—not many young bucks would give a thought to such things when tempted by the offering at Tattersall's. There was also something in the young man's demeanor that kept reminding him of Jeremy—so much so that it was painful. He turned away, pretending not to notice Justin's discomfiture. A chestnut hunter caught his eye, one that was not fifteen hands, but a compact horse with nice lines and sound legs. A good mount, if not spectacular.

"Have you inquired about the chestnut?"

Justin's eyes flared in admiration when he caught sight of the animal in question. "No, sir. I'm sure he's way above my means."

"What do you have to spend?"

Justin told him the figure. The earl was careful to show no reaction to the ridiculously paltry sum. Contrary to what he had told Alex, he did remember what it was like to be young and without funds.

"I am acquainted with the dealer. Perhaps if I have a word with him, I might arrange a favorable price for you."

Justin's face betrayed the war between his longing to acquire a good mount and his reluctance to accept a favor from someone he wanted to dislike. His shoulders stiffened as youthful pride won out. "There is no need to put yourself out, my lord," he replied.

Branford raised an eyebrow at the young man as he stood negligently tapping his crop against the side of his boot. "Mr. Chilton, I am merely offering to help you acquire a decent horse, nothing more," he said pointedly. "If you don't wish to accept, it is of no matter to me."

He turned as if to walk away.

Justin colored at having had his thoughts so easily read. And besides, he *had* been rude, when the man had already saved him from making a big mistake. "My lord," he called "I'm—I'm sorry for my bad manners. I should be very grateful if you would speak to the dealer."

"You are showing some sense, Chilton. By the way, be advised that one doesn't come to Tattersall's the first couple of times without someone experienced to show you how things are done."

Justin swallowed. "I shall remember that, sir."

"Wait here." Branford strolled over to the dealer and,

taking his elbow, guided him out of the young man's hearing. "Miller, how much are you asking for the chestnut?"

The man rubbed his chin. "For you, my lord, fifty guineas."

Branford nodded. "A fair price. Now listen carefully. You will sell the animal to my young friend there. You will tell him the price is twenty pounds. My man of affairs shall send you the rest this afternoon. But if you breathe a word to anyone that I had anything to do with the purchase, you will never see any of my business again. Is that clear?"

The man's head bobbed. "Oh yes, sir. Very."

"Good."

Branford stood aside as Miller hurried over to Justin. In a few minutes the matter was settled, money had changed hands, and Justin's face was beaming with elation. He approached the earl with a huge grin on his face. "Sir, thank you. I am well aware that without your help I would never have gotten such a good price."

Branford smiled to himself, happy that the young man was too green to realize it was an absurd price.

"I never dreamed to own such a horse," continued Justin with boyish enthusiasm. "He is beyond all I could hope for! Of course, he is nothing compared to your magnificent black stallion, Hades. I have seen you ride him in the park—he goes like the wind . . ." Justin trailed off, feeling a fool for blubbering on so to the earl. His expression was one that indicated he expected a cutting set-down.

"Hades is a prime one," agreed Branford pleasantly.

At the earl's friendly tone, Justin recovered his tongue and ventured another question.

"Is it true that he ran at Newcastle in the Haverill Cup?"

"Yes. Came in second by a stride. Strained a hock that made him unfit for racing, but he suits me."

Justin gave a low whistle. "He must have cost a veritable fortune in any case."

"No more than I could afford. Speaking of which, you should have enough left over to be able to see to it that your sister has her new gown as well." He paused for a fraction. "Just make sure it is dark green rather than mauve," he added under his breath.

Justin looked as if he was about to say sharp, then reconsidered, "Green?"

"A very deep green—I am accorded to have an excellent eye for matters of fashion as well as horseflesh."

"It is my aunt who likes mauve," mused Justin, half to himself. "Alex never bothers to overrule her."

"It may very well suit your aunt. It does not suit your sister." He thought for a moment. "If you wish to make a special present to her, you should go to Lady Marie's on Bond Street and trust her choice of style—she is the best modiste in town. Mention my name and she will see you get a favorable price." He made a mental note to send his man around with a full purse to the dressmaker as well as the horse dealer.

Justin nodded. "Thank you for the advice, sir."

"You might also look into new tack—and check it carefully before you ride. It would disturb your family greatly were you to suffer another accident."

The young man's jaw tightened. "I'm sorry Alex felt the need to air her concerns. She gets rather overwrought on the subject, as females are wont to do, when there is nothing to be upset about."

"Your sister does not strike me as the hysterical type, Chilton," replied Branford dryly. "Have you any enemies?"

Justin shook his head, a look of bafflement on his face. "I can think of no reason anyone would have a quarrel with me, much less wish me harm. I'm afraid my life has been rather tame, to say the least." His eyes flicked up shyly to meet the earl's. "Not nearly as interesting as yours."

"You should wish it to stay that way," snapped Branford. "Therefore, I suggest you have a care when you go out so that your sister has no reason to be upset further."

"I will, sir," promised Justin.

The young man excused himself to join a pair of friends he had spotted in the crowd, no doubt to share with them his remarkable good fortune.

The earl's crop tapped at his boot with a little more force. He was not a great believer in coincidence. Yet if it were not coincidence then the accidents befalling young Chilton seemed to make no sense.

And that, in his experience, was the time to be concerned.

Chapter Four

The man stopped his pacing only long enough to pour a large glass of brandy. His fingers played with the knot of his cravat as if to loosen its folds before he resumed walking back and forth in front of the fire.

"Sit down, Arthur. You are acting like a cat on a griddle." The low voice came from a figure seated in a large, overstuffed wing chair, his booted feet propped nonchalantly in front of him. "You are becoming skittish over nothing."

"Bloody hell, I wish we could have done with it, that's all," muttered Standish. "Things are getting riskier—someone might have seen me near Chilton's horse. It was bad enough in the country around that damnable, moldering farm." He took another gulp. "And I don't know why you had to drag Branford, of all people, into this."

Hammerton regarded his cousin through half-closed eyes. "It's nothing to be concerned about. It would have made things easier had he risen to our bait and ruined the girl so that the family would have been forced to return to Sussex. But it is of no matter, believe me. I have things well in hand."

"But I've noticed him dancing with the chit lately, and even conversing with her!"

"Come now." Hammerton smiled. "Do you think the earl is developing a tendre for a plain bluestocking with no family, and poor as a churchmouse in the bargain?" He gave a harsh laugh. "Really!"

Standish let out a breath. "All right, I suppose I am being absurd. But I don't like having him involved in the least."

"Does the earl frighten you?"

Standish dropped his gaze to the floor.

"You see, Arthur, that is why you should leave the thinking to me. Branford will not pose a problem, that I promise you."

"Then let us get it done, by God, and as quickly as possible."

Hammerton shot him a look of contempt. "It will be done, but in such a manner that no suspicion will ever fall at our door. You do not fancy the noose, do you? I for one, do not."

Standish swallowed hard, then drained the rest of his glass in one gulp. "Maybe we don't have to get rid of him at all," he said nervously. "I mean, he has no idea! His father never had a chance to—"

"No, he has no inkling, nor do any of them. But I've always told you he would have to be eliminated someday. Now that he has come to town, the chances, however slim, increase that he might somehow stumble onto the truth."

"Hell and damnation," swore Standish as he grabbed for the bottle on the mahogany sideboard.

"Come now, Arthur. Think on it. Are you really willing to forgo all that you have enjoyed these past years? How long do you think you would be welcome at your clubs, your gaming hells, the beds of your various mistresses, and all the other pleasures you indulge in without the steady stream of money I provide from the Hammerton fortune? Remember where it comes from and think well, cousin. It is a little late to be developing a conscience—or feet of clay." The voice was soft but there was no mistaking the note of warning.

"I've done all you've asked of me," he shot back. "I'm the one who's taken the risks, so don't bloody worry about me. I'm not backing off."

"Good." Hammerton gazed into the fire and swirled his own drink. Standish would have to be watched, he thought. But then he always was a loose screw. He would have to be dealt with at some point in time, but not until he had served his purpose. "As for Branford, he may have unwittingly helped us in a different way than I had planned, but one that may be even more useful. I understand he helped the pup get into Manton's. It is the perfect place for me to strike up an acquaintance with him, become a friendly confidant. It will give me a chance to pick just the right opportunity." His eyes narrowed, the coldness in them sending a chill through even such a hardened jade as Standish.

"The next accident, I promise you, Arthur, will be the last."

"Well," said the soft, throaty voice, "it is about time you finally put in an appearance." A delicate white hand patted the plump down cushion in a meaningful manner. "Come, sit down here beside me."

Branford smiled as he crossed the elegant drawing room. "When you issue a summons, I dare not ignore it." He settled his tall, muscular form onto the sofa and casually stretched one arm up along its back.

"Fustian," retorted the lady sitting next to him with a matching smile. "You know as well as I that you do whatever you please."

He gave a low chuckle. "Tell me," he said bending lower toward her ear, "is your husband at home?"

"Is that how you begin?" exclaimed Lady Ashton. "It seems a rather unimaginative way to start a flirtation."

"No," he admitted. "I do try to be slightly more creative than that."

They both laughed, the comfortable laugh of good friends. Lady Ashton rang for the maid to bring the tea tray.

"I haven't seen you in an age," she said, her expression growing serious. "How are you—truly?"

Branford's expression changed too. "Cecelia, I take it that Henry has been voicing his concerns to you as well, but I should appreciate it if you wouldn't ring a peal over my head too."

Her eyes clouded with concern, "No, I shall leave it to Henry to chide you over the amount of brandy you have been consuming and the . . . other activities. What I care about is you finding some sort of happiness, Sebastian, and I can't believe that what you are doing to yourself will be of any help."

The earl's mouth tightened.

She saw it, but went on regardless. "You have always loved Riverton. You should make it your home, not waste your time—"

"Ah, and how would you have me do that? Would you prefer that I leg-shackle myself to some young lady on the Marriage Mart anxious for a title and fortune?" he asked with a touch of bitterness. "I am well aware of what is expected of me. Are you too going to tell me that it is time to set up my nursery."

"No. And certainly some girl fresh from the schoolroom would not be at all right for you, but"—she sighed—"is there no one you care for?"

He stiffened perceptibly and his arm came down from its casual position on the back of the sofa. "Cecelia, let us drop this now, if you please."

Lady Ashton patted his hand. "Very well."

She was smart enough to know when to pull back from a frontal assault.

The tea tray arrived and she poured them both a cup.

"I didn't realize you had developed such an interest in botany," she remarked as she offered him a plate of assorted cakes.

He declined.

"I understand you drove Miss Chilton to Kew Gardens," she continued with an innocent air, taking two of the pastries herself. "Henry took me last week. The new specimens are marvelous, are they not?"

"Quite." There was a hint of suspicion in Branford's eyes at the direction in which Lady Ashton was marshaling the conversation.

"I imagine Miss Chilton found them fascinating as well. I understand she is an artist with an interest in . . ."

The conversation turned to plants and the exhibition. Despite his initial reluctance, he found himself discussing the various things they had seen and describing Miss Chilton's reactions. He was even led to admit that he had enjoyed the outing more than he had expected.

Lady Ashton polished off her cakes. Then she guided the conversation back to the topic she really wanted to discuss. "You know, I find Miss Chilton extremely interesting."

She gave Branford no time to comment. "It is rare that one can actually have an intelligent conversation during all those tedious afternoon visits and teas and—you men wouldn't know about such things, though Henry does say that some of the gentlemen at your clubs can be dead bores."

That drew a smile from Branford.

"Anyway, it has been pleasant to have an exchange with someone who has an opinion on something rather than just proses on about the weather or the refreshments at the last ball or whether a certain lady looks well in red."

"She *does* have an opinion on things," agreed Branford.

"Well, I look forward to getting to know her better."

Satisfied that her objectives had been achieved by making an oblique foray, she withdrew for the day. Picking up a silver bell on the table, she rang for the butler.

"Now that we have had our little chat I know Henry is looking forward to joining us for tea."

Branford took a sip from his cup. His soldier's instincts were telling him something. He wasn't quite sure how, but he had the distinct feeling that Lady Ashton had managed to outflank him.

Two shots rang out.

The grizzled man scratched at the stubble on his jaw and gave a low whistle. "That be as nice a piece of shooting as I've seen in a while, guv."

Branford allowed himself a slight smile. A low murmur ran through a small group of onlookers, some of whom were bold enough to nod in appreciation at the sight of the two wildly moving targets shattered within seconds of each other.

"Thank you, Lizard. From you, high praise indeed."

The earl slowly lowered the two pistols, savoring the exquisite balance of the deadly-looking weapons. He turned to where an ebony box inlaid with brass lay open, revealing an interior of deep forest velvet. After running a piece of chamois over the burled walnut and polished steel barrels, he placed the pistols in their compartments and snapped the lid shut. The gentlemen lounging around the area parted with alacrity as Branford strolled away, Lizard at his shoulder.

"Young pup you sent over ain't half bad. Raw, but willing ta learn, which is more 'n one can say about most of them's of quality," He jerked his head toward where Justin Chilton was facing a setup of stationary targets. "I sent Jasper over to give him a few pointers."

Branford left off putting on his jacket and watched for a few moments.

Justin reloaded and squeezed off a shot. It caught the paper target, but wide left of the small circle at the center.

"Has Jasper remarked on your stance?"

The young man turned quickly, a look of surprise on his face.

"Try a little more weight on your left foot, then open your right side a touch."

Justin took up his position and Jasper handed him the reloaded gun. This time the bullet was much closer to the mark, though still off-center.

"And relax your hand—you are not strangling a chicken," remarked Branford dryly. He stepped forward. "Here, let me see the pistol."

Justin handed it to him with a slight hesitation. It was at least twenty years old and heavy as a lump of coal. The barrel was pitted from the elements, and as he sighted down the barrel, he could only imagine what the rifling inside looked like. Though someone had recently gone to great pains to bring the gun up to snuff, it was a wonder the thing actually fired, much less hit anything. Branford moved it around in the air, as if testing its balance. Then he laid it aside.

"Try this." He motioned for Lizard to bring his case, then removed one of his own pistols from the soft folds of velvet. He loaded it with practiced ease and handed it to Justin. The young man took it gingerly, eyeing its craftsmanship and obvious quality with something akin to awe.

Branford gestured at the target.

Justin swallowed, then turned and took aim, careful to follow all of the advice the earl had just given him. With the slightest of pressure on the trigger, he fired a shot.

"Dead center." Jasper grinned as he consulted the target. "Yer lordship will be putting me poor self outta a job."

The staff at Manton's treated the earl with an obvious respect, but showed no fear in engaging in easy banter with him.

The corners of Branford's mouth twitched slightly.

Justin fingered the polished wood and chaised silver longingly before he handed the weapon back to the earl. "Thank you, sir. I'm—I'm grateful for your pointers—and for the chance to use such a fine piece." His eyes unconsciously followed the pistol's progress back into its case.

Branford nodded. He handed the other gun back to Justin, who grimaced slightly at its awkward weight.

"Yours?" asked the earl.

The young man colored slightly and raised his chin—a gesture Branford was becoming well used to. The earl felt a twinge of sympathy for Justin's embarrassment. He remembered well enough what it was like to be short of funds but have a surfeit of youthful pride.

"It belonged to my father," replied Justin stiffly. "I haven't . . . purchased one of my own yet."

"There is no shame in lacking blunt, Chilton. And no need to act as if there is," murmured Branford, in a voice low enough that only Justin could hear. Then, in a louder tone he added. "Jasper, see to it that Mr. Chilton shoots with a decent gun on his next visit. Good day."

Before Justin could utter any further words, he was already staring at the earl's back. He shook his head slightly, perplexed. His good friend, Frederick Hartley, had witnessed the encounter and rushed over, his eyes wide with astonishment.

"Good lord, Justin. The Icy Earl actually spoke to you!" Hartley's voice was tinged with awe. "And not only that—he offered you one of his matched pair!"

"Ain't never seen the likes o' that," said Jasper, shooting Justin an appraising look. "Nope. Ain't never seen him offer one o' his barking irons to nobody."

The two young men gathered their things and made to leave.

"Thursday at one, Mr. Chilton," added Jasper.

Justin nodded, then he and Hartley walked off, drawing not a few interested glances.

"I didn't know you were acquaintances," persisted Hartley, as they walked toward his phaeton.

"Hardly at all. That is, he—he is a friend of Alex," mumbled Justin. "They share a mutual interest in botany," he added quickly, lest Hartley get the wrong idea.

Disregarding Justin's disavowal, Hartley looked at him with newfound respect. "Wait until Stanford and Yorkhill hear about this! They'll be green with envy that they missed it."

Justin colored slightly. "It's nothing to make a fuss over, really, Freddy. I daresay he was merely . . ."

Merely what? Justin found he had no idea. Somehow the idea that the earl was trying to cozen up to him was absurd—but equally absurd was the idea that he was acting in . . . friendship.

"I say," exclaimed Hartley, taking no notice that Justin's voice had trailed off. "The others will be most impressed—egad! I nearly forgot!" He hastily consulted his gold pocketwatch. "I am supposed to attend on my grandmother at one, without fail." His face took on a pained expression. "She is having guests—including a chit of marriageable age, no doubt. But as she grants me a most generous allowance, I must do my duty. I fear it means abandoning you here."

Justin laughed. "You go on. It is a pleasant day. I shall walk."

Indeed, he was still new enough to town to find the streets fascinating. A myriad of sights, smells, and sounds overwhelmed his senses—the cries of a costermonger, the pungent yeastiness of a spilled keg of ale, the smart carriages with matched teams jostling with dray carts. He was so lost in his observations that it took a second greeting to catch his attention.

"Mr. Chilton."

Justin's head snapped up. "I beg your pardon. I fear I was woolgathering."

"So it seems." There was a faint smile on Branford's face as he controlled his spirited team with careless ease. "Do you go on to Half Moon Street? I am passing by there if you care to climb up."

Justin hesitated.

The horses danced with impatience.

"They are getting cold while you ponder the offer. If you prefer to walk . . ." He made as if to give the team its head.

Realizing how rude he was appearing, Justin quickly made his decision.

"Thank you, sir," he said as he climbed up beside the earl.

Branford flicked the whip and they were off.

They rode in silence for a bit, with Justin casting surreptitious looks to observe just how the earl handled the ribbons. After all, it wasn't every day that he had the chance to ride with a nonpareil, a member of the Four-in-Hand Club, and he was determined to learn any little trick he could.

Branford suppressed a smile at the young man's obvious

interest and smartly guided the team around a number of slower moving conveyances, displaying a number of skillful moves with the whip and reins. It gave him an odd twinge as he recalled how his young cousin had sat with him, showing much the same rapt attention as Alex's brother. Yet he found that he was rather enjoying himself—he had to admit it was nice to see admiration rather than fear in another's eye.

"Tell me, Chilton," he said after a while. "What was your father like?"

Justin started in surprise. "What?"

"What sort of man was he?" Noticing the young man's consternation, he added a brief explanation. "Your sister asked me to look at—"

"The infamous letter," groaned Justin.

"Quite."

"I'm sorry, sir, that she saw fit to pester you with such nonsense. You needn't take it seriously."

"I take my word very seriously, Chilton. And I promised your sister I would endeavor to help. Now, it's an unusual sort of system he's devised. Sometimes someone with no training in the subject is tougher to crack than one who follows set principles or patterns. In my experience, it helps to know something about the person himself. Little things may help provide a key as to how a person thinks."

Justin nodded slowly. "I think I see what you mean." He thought for a moment. "He was a . . . driven man, wrapped up in his own world. I mean, he was kind enough to us, but, well, even as a child I sensed there was a part of him he wouldn't share. At times, he would fall into dark moods—that was when he would go off on one of his trips, to gather material on his book. When he returned, things would usually be fine for a while. Until the next mood." He seemed to be struggling with painful memories. "Alex had to take care of all the practical things, for our mother died when I was very young. I—I wish I could have helped her more." He caught himself. "I daresay this probably sounds quite ridiculous to you."

"Not at all," said Branford quietly.

Justin let out a breath. He had not made a cake of himself, then. More than that, he somehow sensed an understanding in the earl that made him not regret having made such private revelations.

The carriage had arrived in front of the modest town house Lady Beckworth had taken for the Season. As Justin made to dismount, he turned impulsively to Branford. "Would you care to come in for tea, sir? It is nothing out of the ordinary, but . . ."

He hesitated, suddenly feeling rather gauche—one didn't ask the Icy Earl to tea!

It was Branford's turn to hesitate, a look of surprise flitting across his normally impassive features.

"I believe I would."

He tossed the reins to his tiger, giving directions for the horses to be cooled down, then followed Justin up the stairs. An elderly butler took their hats and walking sticks, and Justin immediately headed for the library. Instead of waiting in the drawing room, as Justin had offered, Branford followed along.

"Alex, Aunt Aurelia, we have a guest for tea."

Alex didn't lift her eyes from her easel. She wore a shapeless smock over her gown, and a large paintbrush was stuck behind her ear. It had dislodged a number of hairpins so that her thick tresses hung down in a bit of disarray on one side. A smudge of cerulean blue stood out on her cheekbone, the result of her constantly pushing the strands aside with the handle of the brush.

"What time is it?" she demanded, the annoyance at being

interrupted quite evident in her tone. "Can't you send whoever it is away?" Then, as she looked up, she added, "Oh!" in little more than a squeak.

Branford walked deliberately toward the easel.

"My lord—" she began.

He ignored her and came around to view the painting. "Hmmmm." He cocked his head to one side.

Alex put down the brush she was using and jabbed at her errant locks. "It is most disconcerting to be interrupted in the middle of my work. I told you, I do not make a habit of showing a work in progress—"

"It is progressing very nicely."

"It is extremely ungentlemanly to barge in uninvited," she countered.

Branford's eyebrows rose. "But I *was* invited."

Alex looked startled. She looked from the earl to her brother, then down to her own paint-spattered smock. Her hand flew once more to her hair in dismay as she realized the picture she must be presenting.

"If you will excuse me, I shall inform Cook that there will be one more for tea." She hurried from the room.

"Aunt Aurelia"—Justin called in a loud voice to get his aunt's attention—"Lord Branford is to join us for tea."

"Oh."

Branford had to strain to make out the diminutive gray head that was barely visible from behind an enormous moroccan-bound book.

"How nice." She smiled vaguely in their direction as she let the volume close with a thud. "He isn't going to shoot anyone today, is he?"

Justin sucked in his breath.

"Rest assured, madam, I shall endeavor not to put a period to anyone's existence for the next hour," answered the earl with a twitch of his lips.

"My lord," said Justin in a low voice, tight with embarrassment. "I must apologize for my family's odd manners. It would be completely understandable if you wish to reconsider . . ."

A look of unholy amusement glinted in Branford's eyes. "Wouldn't dream of it, Chilton. I'm already enjoying myself immensely." To Justin's further surprise, the earl broke into what could only be described as a broad grin.

An hour later, Justin found he was amazed about a good deal of other things. Branford reviewed the upcoming races at Newcastle with him, adding some very pithy anecdotes concerning the jockeys due to ride. He discussed Homer with his aunt, delighting the older lady by quoting passages in the original Greek. He also discussed—or argued, really—the aesthetics of garden design with his sister, seeming in no way taken aback by her strong opinions and vocal espousing of them. True to his word, he did seem, despite Justin's fears to the contrary, to be enjoying himself.

"What fustian," snapped Alex in reply to an observation the earl had just made. "That is a typically male point of view—if there is a rock where you want a tree, simply dump a barrel of gunpowder on it and get rid of it."

Branford regarded her thoughtfully. "And what, pray tell, would be a typical female reaction?"

"A female would look at the rock and the surroundings and consider whether the rock might work in harmony with a different arrangement of plantings and whether the tree might look just as well in another spot."

The earl's eyes crinkled in amusement. "And you, Miss Chilton, be honest. Would you settle for a rock in your garden?"

Alex smiled in spite of herself. "Quite likely not," she admitted.

"I rather thought not. I think you would inform the rock

of all the reasons its presence was unacceptable there and it would take itself off of its own accord."

Justin let out a peal of laughter. "You have the right of it, sir," he said, ignoring Alex's indignant expression. "Why, I could tell you some tales of what Alex did—"

"Justin! I'm sure his lordship is not interested in such childish nonsense."

"Remember the time you and Father—" Justin stopped and a pensive look clouded the laughter from his features. "Lord Branford was asking me earlier about Father, what sort of a man he was." He looked over at the earl. "Perhaps you should ask Alex and Aunt Aurelia as well, sir."

Alex shot a quick glance at Branford too. "You are thinking of the code?"

He nodded.

She thought for a bit. "Papa shared his passion for his work with us—his love of flora and fauna—but little of his private thoughts. He was very remote at times, even angry, though I could never imagine at what. For the most part he was—"

"He was a very troubled man."

Everyone turned to look at Lady Beckworth.

"I don't know quite why he married your mother," she continued. "Forgive me if I cause the two of you any pain, but I believe you are both of an age where you will understand what I am saying. Oh, he cared for Olivia and the two of you, but it was as if it were merely accommodating his . . . daily needs."

"It does not sound a great deal different than many marriages," observed Branford softly.

She nodded at him, acknowledging his quick insight. "Too true, my lord. But it was not mere indifference or indulgence. Something was eating at him inside. Something he wouldn't share with anyone."

"How did Mama feel about it?" asked Alex.

"At first I believe she thought she could change him. Later, she accepted what part of himself he could give. As you know, he was never deliberately cruel."

But blindly selfish, thought Branford with an inward frown, to saddle a young daughter with the burdens of an adult. He noticed that Lady Beckworth's grip tightened on her teacup as she went on.

"I thought the fact that he let the responsibility of running a household and managing Justin fall on you at such an age outside of enough."

"I didn't mind," said Alex quietly. "And we had a very interesting time growing up, learning a variety of things, seeing different places as he worked on his *Natural History of England.*"

"There is more to life than work and I shall always be cross with him for failing to realize that with his own children," replied Lady Beckworth, her tone gentle yet edged in anger.

"What of his family? What were his parents, his siblings like?"

Both Alex and Justin looked blank.

"He never spoke of them, ever. It was as if they . . . didn't exist," said Justin.

The earl looked questioningly at their aunt.

She shook her head too. "I remember him telling Olivia that his family was—gone. He seemed unwilling to discuss the matter so she never pushed him further."

Branford looked slightly askance.

"Yes," acknowledged Lady Beckworth. "I suppose it sounds strange. But he was a respectable young man, introduced to Olivia by a friend of our family. It didn't seem so terribly important."

"So you have no idea where he was from?"

Lady Beckworth shook her head.

"You know, I hadn't really thought about it," mused Alex, "but in all our travels, Papa never once mentioned that we were near where he grew up or some such thing as that. And we went nearly everywhere."

"Except East Anglia," pointed out Justin. "Said he hated the fens. Said it chilled him to the bone."

Branford looked questioningly at Alex. "But I thought that is where you said he was when he had his accident?"

"Ironic, isn't it?" she replied. "It was his first trip there. I imagine he knew he had to visit it at some time if he wished to finish his *Natural History*. After all, he couldn't very well leave it out."

It was a rational explanation, but something he couldn't lay a finger on was bothering Branford.

"Does any of this help?" asked Alex.

"I'm not sure," answered the earl frankly. "I shall have to think on it."

But he had little time to mull over it at the present. The clock on the mantelpiece chimed the hour, causing him to put aside his cup and rise from the comfortable but worn wing chair.

"I fear I have lost track of the time. As I am engaged for the evening, I regret that I must take my leave." He bowed gracefully to Lady Beckworth, taking her frail hand and pressing it lightly to his lips.

She smiled warmly. "I hope you shall call again, Lord Branford."

"You may count on it."

"And don't forget to bring that volume of Aristophanes you mentioned."

"Ah," he gave a mock grimace. "And I thought it was my scintillating conversation that had garnered the invitation."

As Lady Beckworth let out a laugh, he nodded to the two young people and took his leave.

A companionable silence reigned in the small drawing room as they each sat engaged with their own thoughts. Then suddenly Lady Beckworth lifted her head, her mouth set in a determined line. "Fools," she announced. "Utter fools."

Alex and Justin exchanged puzzled looks.

"Who?" ventured Alex.

"Society! How such stupid rumors start is beyond me." She snapped her book shut. "Why, to listen to the *ton,* you'd think the man was Lucifer incarnate. I may be in my dotage, but I find his lordship delightful—witty, charming, intelligent, with a sense of humor as well." She gave a little sigh. "If I were fifty years younger, I should set my cap for him."

Alex rattled one of the cups she was stacking on the tea tray. Though she had rearranged her hair before coming back downstairs, it had loosened once again, falling just enough to hide her expression.

Lord Branford glanced in the large gilt mirror that hung in the entrance hall of his town house and straightened the cravat of his evening dress. Picking up his hat and cane from the polished side table, he gave a brief nod to the footman who quietly materialized from the shadows to open the stately front door. His carriage was already waiting at the bottom of the steps, but instead of climbing in, he walked around to the mews. Inside, a short, stocky groom was putting away a newly cleaned harness. So deft were his movements that it would have taken most people more than a few moments to notice he worked with only one hand. His left shirt sleeve was sewn shut to cover a stump that ended at the wrist.

"Evening, Sykes."

Sykes nodded. "Cap'n."

"I have a special job for you."

The man's eyes lit up with interest.

Branford handed him some folded sheets of paper. "This explains what I want you to do. Be ready to leave for East Anglia first thing in the morning. Simms will arrange a horse."

"Aye, Cap'n." The ex-soldier still had not lost the habit of addressing his former officer in military terms.

"I needn't remind you that this is a matter of great discretion."

The man spit into the hay.

Branford gave a slight smile. "No, I thought not." He placed a heavy leather purse on top of the stall door. "Expense is no object. And keep me informed of anything you discover."

Sykes gave a quick salute with his good hand.

"Good night, then."

Alex surveyed the crowded ballroom. At least there was a possibility of some interesting conversation, she noted, spying Mr. Simpson and a group of other Botanical Society members clustered around a rather overblown display of orchids at the far end of the room. Just then, the music struck up and she was obliged to wait until the dance was over before making her way across the floor. As the gentlemen in their evening dress and ladies swathed in expensive silks capered through the lively steps of a country dance, she noted, not for the first time, that Branford had not made an appearance at any of the entertainments she had attended over the past number of days. In fact, she had not seen him for more than a week.

Alex found herself wondering what other engagements

he had, with whom he spent his evenings. An elegant lady paused in front of her, laughing in a light trill at something her partner had just said. Her graceful fingers pressed against the milky skin revealed by a low-cut gown as she lowered her eyes and murmured something softly in reply. The smoldering look the lady received from the gentleman made Alex just a little bit envious. She knew she couldn't—nay, wouldn't want to—perfect the art of coquetry in a millennium. But she couldn't help but think it would be interesting to inspire such a look from a man.

Was that the sort of lady Lord Branford took to his bed? Oh, she was, as she had informed the earl, quite aware of what went on in the bedroom—well, most of it, that is. Did he look at a lady that way as he was unfastening—

She caught herself and colored slightly, grateful that no one could read her highly improper thoughts.

Drat the man, anyway!

Why had he popped into her thoughts yet again when all she really wanted to do was concentrate on her work? The hibiscus—*his* hibiscus, she reminded herself—was turning out better than she had ever imagined. With just a few more—

"Alex! There you are."

She came out of her reverie with a jolt. Up came her head to see her brother approaching, accompanied by another gentleman. He was of medium height and very elegantly dressed, though his waistcoat was overly bright for Alex's taste and had an excess of fobs dangling in a conspicuous manner.

"Alex, I should like you to meet a new acquaintance of mine, his lordship the Earl of Hammerton. Hammerton, my sister Alexandra."

The man bowed low over Alex's hand. "A pleasure, Miss Chilton. Your brother has spoken of what an authority you are on plants. I wonder if I may be so bold as to ask your advice on a garden design for one of my estates?"

"I should be happy to try, but it is really not my field of expertise—"

Hammerton cut her off. "Chilton, you are a sly one. You neglected to mention that your sister was lovelier than any summer rose."

Alex imagined it was a well-turned compliment, one that should please any lady. But there was something she couldn't quite identify that put her off about the man. However, he appeared to be a friend of Justin's. She smiled politely.

"Perhaps if you are free for the next dance?" He phrased it as a question though he was already extending his hand for her arm. There was nothing short of appearing rude that she could do so she placed her hand on the proffered arm and followed him onto the dance floor. Besides, if he had an interest in gardens, he must be a pleasant enough fellow despite her initial misgivings.

To her mild surprise, when he began to speak it was not of his own concerns.

"I trust your brother has fully recovered from his unfortunate accident?" he inquired. "I was most shocked to hear about it."

"Yes, he is quite well, thank goodness."

Hammerton shook his head in exaggerated concern. "From what I hear, he could have been seriously hurt in the mishap."

Alex's throat tightened. "Yes."

"What a shame. He is such an amiable young man. I hope I may be of assistance in introducing him to the proper people and places here in town. I remember what it was like to be new. It's so easy to be led astray."

Alex felt a surge of gratitude. Perhaps she had misjudged him after all. It was a generous offer from an earl.

"I have heard that is true, my lord. I should be very grateful if you would keep an eye on him and see he is . . . kept out of danger."

"Danger? Surely you cannot mean to imply that was anything but chance!" Hammerton's voice seemed to convey disbelief, even a little mockery. "Or perhaps you exaggerate, as most females are wont to do. After all, young men are bound to take a spill or two."

Alex's opinion of him plummeted once more.

"It was not only this particular incident, Lord Hammerton," she said sharply. "This was not the first accident."

His eyes seemed to doubt her. "Really?"

She felt goaded. "Yes, really. There have been other occurrences. And not only that, I am of the opinion that his saddle's girth was deliberately tampered with."

An emotion flashed across Hammerton's face before he quickly brought himself under control. "That *is* something to be concerned about. What does your brother think about such disturbing news?"

"He thinks I am overreacting."

"Well, no doubt you *are* mistaken, Miss Chilton," he said smoothly. "After all, what possible reason could someone have for wanting to harm your brother?"

Alex sighed in frustration. "That is what I cannot figure out. But I plan on doing some investigations of my own. I intend to get to the bottom of the matter."

Hammerton gave her a smile. "I shouldn't dwell on it overly. A young lady most certainly has other, more important things to occupy her thoughts. I'm sure that your brother will be taken care of."

As the music was coming to a close, Alex indicated that she wished to be escorted to where her friends were gathered around the orchids. "In fact," she said as they made their way across the floor, "it is Mr. Simpson who is very knowledgeable on gardens. I am certain he would be happy to advise—"

"Yes, I shall be sure to consult him later regarding the plans," said Hammerton. "But I fear I have another engagement right now that I must attend to. Perhaps later." He bowed politely. "I look forward to meeting again, Miss Chilton."

Sooner than you think, he added to himself.

Chapter Five

The brush moved deftly, laying in a subtle shading of deep alizarin crimson to create a delicate shadow under the curling petals of the flower. Satisfied, Alex put aside her palette and stepped back to assess the work as a whole. Even she had to admit it had turned out rather well.

What would the earl do with it? Would it hang somewhere those bright, sapphire eyes would observe it regularly? Or would he quickly tire of it, as Society said he was wont to do with most things, and consign it to some moldy attic? She sighed. There was precious little say she had on that score. Somehow, however, it would be nice to think the flash of regard she had caught in his eye was no mere passing fancy, that he did not discard things that he admired quite so readily. Carefully unfastening the thick, textured sheet of paper from her easel, Alex carried the finished painting over to the table. She untied the ribbons of her portfolio and slid it inside.

Well, at least she was ready to fulfill her end of the business arrangement.

The letter. Her lips pursed at the thought. Had she made a cake of herself in asking him to spend what may turn out to be hours on deciphering the mysterious message? Good heavens, what if it did, in fact, turn out to be naught but a list of plants and where her father had found them? Why, perhaps the strange symbols were not hatchets but hand trowels, the kind he used to dig up his specimens. It might very well be they were only something as mundane as a notation for how difficult the terrain made it to remove them.

Oh dear. She would feel like the veriest of fools. No doubt he should tease her unmercifully—yet the notion didn't seem to bother her unduly. Her gaze drifted toward the tall, leaded-glass windows as she imagined the low, mellifluous voice and those lively blue eyes. . . . Then she shook her head to banish such idle daydreams. The earl had as yet done nothing to fulfill his end of the bargain, she reminded herself. He certainly had given the problem no further thought, for she had heard nothing from him this past week. Perhaps he had forgotten about it after all.

With a determined expression, she took up a fresh piece of paper and a stick of charcoal. Really, it was time to get back to work.

Her friends were engaged in an animated conversation concerning the last week's lecture. Mr. Graves, a noted expert on roses, had stirred up a great deal of controversy with his theories on hybrids, due in no small part to his abrasive manner. Normally Alex would have thrown herself wholeheartedly into the fray, but tonight she found her attention wandering.

Her thoughts strayed to more pressing concerns than those of shape and color. Though she was ready to complete her end of the business deal with the earl, she had been bothered since this afternoon by the realization that she had done nothing to follow up on her own vow to investigate the accidents. It was difficult to know where to begin, having little practice in this sort of thing—but of course she would never admit that to him. Her jaw set at the memory of his words advising her to drop the whole matter.

She had only to apply logic to the problem, she told herself. Her mind set to work. Perhaps a first step would be to find out if any stranger had been seen in the vicinity of the accidents. That was a start, at least. She would write to her aunt's steward first thing in the morning. And she would make a point of questioning Mr. Hartley most thoroughly.

Yes, she would show him she could use her head . . .

She spotted him as soon as he entered the room. His dark evening clothes were in marked contrast to the brighter colors favored by a majority of the gentlemen present. His eyes seemed to sweep the room and she felt a pinch of disappointment when they didn't so much as pause a fraction to acknowledge her presence. When he moved on and was hidden by the crowd near the punch table she sighed inwardly and forced herself to attend to the last of Mr. Simpson's comments.

"Good evening, Miss Chilton."

Alex whirled around at the sound of the familiar, deep voice.

"My lord." Though she tried to keep her tone neutral, her face came alight with pleasure at seeing him. "Why, where have you been this past week?"

The words popped out of her mouth before she realized what she was saying.

"Ah, has my presence been missed, then?" There was a twinkle in his eye.

She felt a blush stealing over her and ducked her head to hide a rush of embarrassment. "No, of course not—I mean . . ." she said, struggling to regain her equilibrium. "It's just that I have been wondering about our . . . business arrangement." She took a deep breath to steady her momentary confusion and was able to continue in a more assured manner. "Well? Have you made any progress?"

"I regret that other matters have prevented me from dealing with your problem. Be assured that I will address it forthwith."

Alex found herself wondering just what had occupied the earl's attention for more than a week.

"I trust you have been well?" Branford asked pleasantly, seeming to ignore the awkward interchange that had just taken place.

"Quite." To her consternation, she felt the blush returning. Good Lord, she berated herself angrily. She was acting worse than a giddy schoolroom miss. Whatever had come over her?

"Is something wrong?"

Alex's head snapped up. "Why do you ask?"

"Because the scowl on your face would put Marshal Nye to rout."

"Oh. Sorry," she mumbled. "I was thinking of something else."

He took her arm familiarly. "Well, I shall endeavor to keep your thoughts turned to less disturbing things than they are dwelling on now. I trust you will allow me the next dance?"

Before she could compose herself for a reply, they passed Justin and a petite brown-haired young lady of not more than average looks but dressed expensively in a figured silk gown of the latest fashion.

"Hello, Alex." Her brother greeted her, then smiled rather shyly at the earl as well. "Good evening, Lord Branford. May I have the honor of presenting my friend, Miss Lockwood."

Branford bowed politely. "Miss Lockwood."

The young lady dipped a hurried curtsy, then shied against Justin's shoulder. Words seemed to elude her. Justin's hand tightened on her arm in a reassuring manner. He smiled an encouragement at her downcast face before nodding once more to the two of them. Then he guided her out onto the middle of the dance floor.

"I suppose she does not chatter your brother's ear off," remarked Branford dryly.

Alex had to stifle a grin. "Truly, she is not so addlepated as she just appeared. She is much more at home in the country where she is quite content with her life. She does not like London and feels intimidated by all the machinations of the *ton*—her parents included."

The earl looked at her questioningly.

"Justin and Anne have known each other for ages and are in love. He would like to offer for her, but her father has bigger plans and won't hear of it. With his deep pockets, he is angling for a title—an earl at least though it appears he may have to be content with a mere baron."

"I see."

Alex sighed. "Yes, that's really the main reason we are here for the Season. Justin can't bear to give her up. Somehow he hopes to change her father's mind. But I fear it is rather hopeless."

Branford frowned slightly as his eyes followed the young couple. He looked as if to say something, then merely compressed his lips and led her onto the floor as well.

Miss Lockwood watched the earl lead Alex out. "How can your sister have the nerve to dance with the Icy Earl?" she whispered to Justin. "Why, I'm terrified just looking at him. So tall and dark and forbidding—"

"Why, Lord Branford isn't at all like what they say," Justin found himself saying. "In fact, Alex finds his company quite enjoyable."

Miss Lockwood looked at him doubtfully. "But it is said he . . . is ruthless and cold and, well, not a gentleman."

Justin frowned. "Anne, I should hope you would have more sense than to judge someone by what the gossips say."

His eyes strayed over to the earl. "I, for one, think he is a great gun."

As the music started, Alex was more aware than ever of the light pressure of Branford's hand at her waist, of the strength of his hand around hers as he guided her through the lilting first steps of the waltz. What was the matter with her? she thought. She, who never fell prey to any sort of indisposition, was feeling decidedly odd again—perhaps she should not have had a glass of champagne earlier. That must be it.

"It's back."

Alex started. "What?"

"The frown, Miss Chilton. I fear I am failing in my promise to keep your attention."

"Not at all."

"Why, with that black a look, I should hope I am *not* in your thoughts."

"Why should you be?" she muttered.

Branford laughed softly. "Why indeed." Then he quickened the tempo, giving neither of them the chance to speak for the rest of the dance.

The musicians put aside their instruments for a short break and people began to drift toward the game room and the refreshments. As Alex and Branford paused to allow an animated group of young couples to jostle their way off the dance floor, a tall, voluptuous blonde, her gown cut very low to reveal her obvious charms, motioned her partner to go on while she stopped in front of the earl.

"Why, Sebastian, dear, it has been an age." Her fan of hand-painted Chinese silk tapped lightly on his shoulder and she left it there so that her hand remained touching the immaculately tailored black serge.

"Lady Cameron." Branford nodded slightly.

The lady ignored Alex and stepped closer to him. "Lady

Cameron, indeed!" she said in a low, throaty voice. "Why, there is no need to be so formal, Sebastian. I do hope you will call at Grosvenor Square sometime very soon." Her thick lashes lowered demurely. "George is off on the Continent with Wellington again and it can be so very lonely without one's special friends."

Branford merely bowed a fraction, and in the process managed to dislodge the hand from his shoulder. "How very rag-mannered of me," he said pointedly. "I don't believe you are acquainted with Miss Chilton."

Lady Cameron's gaze slowly raked Alex from head to toe. "How delightful," she said, her voice indicating it was anything but. After a slight pause, she added, "I take it you are new in town. If you would like a recommendation for anything—such as a modiste who is acquainted with the current fashions—I should be happy to oblige." The sneer was barely suppressed.

Alex gritted her teeth to avoid snapping an angry retort.

Lady Cameron unconsciously smoothed the lush figured silk of her exquisite gown. Without another glance at Alex, she turned her attention back to Branford.

"Do not be a stranger. You know you are always welcome. Anytime." With a slight toss of her golden ringlets and one more playful tap of her costly fan, she moved gracefully toward the crowd milling around the punch bowl.

Alex had to stifle the urge to plant a well-aimed kick on the provocatively swaying derriere.

The mood of the evening suddenly changed for her. The glittering lights of the myriad candles seemed too glaring, the scent of the roses too cloying, the notes of the violin too flat, the conversations too shrill.

Her teeth set on edge.

Branford regarded her silently for a few moments. "Are you feeling out of sorts this evening, Miss Chilton?"

Alex was about to let fly with a scathing retort, but instead an entirely different set of words came tumbling out.

"Sometimes I wish I were more like . . . like a Lady Cameron."

"Don't be an idiot," growled Branford. "You are much too sensible to think such nonsense as that."

Alex was stung by his words. "I know I have neither the beauty nor the gowns, nor—"

"That is not what I said!" snapped the earl.

Alex's chin came up defiantly. "Perhaps I am tired of being sensible. Someone like Lady Cameron has a certain charm—"

"She is little more than a courtesan," interrupted Branford. "She offers her charms quite freely—"

"Obviously you speak from experience."

"That, Miss Chilton, is most certainly *not* a topic of conversation open to you." The earl's voice was dangerously soft.

Of course he was quite right, she thought as she turned away from him. But to her consternation, she felt a slight stinging in her eyes.

"Forgive me, my lord," she said coldly. "Naturally you are quite right. Your affairs are none of my concern. Now, if you would kindly return me to my friends, I believe I am engaged with Mr. Duckleigh for the next set."

Branford's mouth set in a tight line as he offered her his arm. They walked across the room in stiff silence and parted without a word.

Charles Duckleigh greeted her warmly, throwing a daggerlike look after the earl as his broad back disappeared into the crowd.

"I wish," he added in a low voice, "that you would not allow that blackguard to hover around you so."

"And *I* wish that everyone would cease advising me on

whom I should and should not speak with or what I should and should not do. I am heartily sick of it. I am neither an imbecile nor a child, Charles. At my age, I am perfectly capable of dealing with the Earl of Branford—or anyone else—without suffering any dire consequences."

Her tone was perhaps sharper than she meant, for Charles reddened and began to stammer an apology.

"Alex, I did not mean to imply—"

She laid a hand on his forearm. "Forgive me, Charles, for shrieking at you like a harridan. I fear I have been rather . . . out of sorts this evening."

Visibly relieved, he straightened his shoulders. "I'm sorry for oversetting you. It is only because . . ." He let his words trail off. "Ah, perhaps you would care to take a walk in the garden instead of dancing?"

Alex nodded gratefully. It seemed like an excellent idea.

The cool evening air felt lovely after the confines of the crowded ballroom. They strolled along a graveled path, admiring the lush plantings that looked even more alluring in the silver wash of moonlight. Alex was so intent on studying a particular bloom of freesia that she didn't notice Charles had slipped his arm around her waist until he pulled her to a stop.

"Alex! My *dear* Alex, I should say. I fear I can no longer contain my feelings . . ."

If she were prone to headaches, she was sure she would have developed one now. What an evening!

"Charles," she said gently, disengaging his arm and turning to face him squarely.

"Please don't interrupt me, else my courage may fail me!"

"Oh, Charles. You are a dear friend, but I should not suit you at all."

He looked perplexed. "But why? I don't understand."

"I am too opinionated, too outspoken, for one."

"I am sure you would learn to temper your feelings—"

"I am sure I would not," she replied firmly. "I assure you, for a man in your position, who hopes to advance in the ministry, I would be a liability."

That gave him pause to think. "But Alex, perhaps—"

"It is truly for the best."

"I—"

The sound of approaching footsteps curtailed any further discussion. A figure appeared from around a boxwood hedge, wreathed in the pungent smoke from a thick cheroot. Its progress was stopped short by the couple in the middle of the path. Alex hastily took a step back from her companion, pulling away from his encircling grasp as Branford exhaled slowly, forming a couple of perfect O's that drifted lazily away in the breeze as he regarded the two of them.

"Is there a new country dance?" he inquired dryly. "One that entails jaunts down garden paths?"

Charles stiffened. "I was just taking Alex—Miss Chilton—back to the ballroom. She was feeling a trifle . . . overheated."

"Good. Then you may take yourself off while she finishes cooling off. I shall escort Miss Chilton back as soon as I have had a word with her."

"I'll not leave Miss Chilton out here in the dark alone—"

"She will not be alone."

Charles stopped, nonplussed. "That is what I meant, sir. Alone with you."

"You seem a trifle confused. If she is with me, she will not be alone," pointed out the earl.

Charles was momentarily speechless, his face betraying a mixture of anger and consternation.

"That's quite enough!" snapped Alex, barely restraining the urge to stamp her foot. "How dare either of you discuss what I may or may not do as if I was not present and capable of making up my own mind."

Charles flushed while Branford's mouth twitched at the corners.

She caught his expression and threw a black look at him before speaking directly to Duckleigh.

"Charles, you may return to the ballroom while I listen to what Lord Branford wishes to say. As a gentleman, he will naturally provide a proper escort back to my friends."

Charles clenched his hands into fists but her words gave him no alternative. "If that is what you wish, Alex, then obviously I shall abide by your decision." He bowed formally to her and, throwing one last glare at the earl, retreated with as much dignity as he could muster.

"Hmmmph," remarked Branford, casually blowing another smoke ring. "Your friend has more gumption than I would have given him credit for."

"His emotions are rather out of check tonight. And no doubt it did not help matters that you interrupted when he was making his declaration—"

Branford choked on a mouthful of smoke.

"What!" he managed to sputter.

"I said, he was asking me to marry him when you—"

"That's ridiculous!"

For the second time during the evening, Alex was stung by his words. "Oh, you think it impossible that someone would wish to marry me?"

"What I meant, Miss Chilton, was that, in my opinion, it would not be a fortuitous match."

"Because Charles lacks a fortune and I am plain?"

"Because he is in awe of you and you would tire of it rather quickly."

She was amazed by how astutely he had divined the very

essence of why she had rejected Charles—but, in her current mood, there was no way she was going to acknowledge it.

"No, what you really meant was that you cannot conceive of a gentlemen being attracted to anyone who does not have long lashes or a well-endowed . . ." She faltered, knowing she was being childish.

"You seem intent on deliberately misunderstanding me this evening," said Branford softly. He dropped his cheroot onto the gravel and ground out the glowing tip with his boot. "Perhaps it would be best if I take you back to your friends." His eyes drifted from her stormy face down a trifle lower and rested there for a moment. "And you have no reason to be jealous of Lady Cameron's endowments."

This time she did stamp her foot. "I am *not* jealous of Lady Cameron!"

He looked at her curiously for a moment before taking her arm. They walked in silence, the only sounds the crunching of their steps on the gravel, until they came to the steps of the terrace leading up to the French doors of the ballroom. The faint sound of conversation and music wafted out.

"By the way," said Branford, drawing them to a halt. "May I be the first to offer my congratulations."

Alex looked at him as if he were speaking Hindu. "What are you talking about?"

"Your impending nuptials, Miss Chilton. I mean to wish you happy."

"Oh, that. Of course I'm not marrying Charles."

"Why not?"

Alex thought for a moment. "That, Lord Branford, is most certainly *not* a topic of conversation open to you."

He made no reply but there was laughter in his eyes as he led her back into the room to join her friends.

* * *

Branford left the ball immediately. Walking amid the crush of carriages, he located his own and waved it home without him. In his current state of mind, he preffered a long walk. If it were June, he thought ruefully, the evening's crosscurrents of emotions might be written off—as the Bard himself had done—as the effects of Midsummer Night's Eve. But in truth, he had no better explanation for the strange way he was feeling.

She had been glad to see him, of that he was sure. He smiled briefly at the recollection of how her eyes had lit up with that mesmerizing mix of hazel and green. It was damnably nice to have someone look at you that way, he mused. But her mood had changed so quixotically! Whatever in the world had made her say such ludicrous things? How could she think to be jealous over a piece of baggage like Lady Cameron—his long legs stopped abruptly in mid-stride.

Jealous.

He came to a halt, his walking stick tapping thoughtfully against his leg. Could it be that she . . . cared that Lady Cameron had all but invited him into her bed? He began walking again. He had to admit the idea had rather intriguing connotations. But remembering her next words was like a dash of cold water. She had made it quite clear his affairs meant nothing to her. He shook his head.

Well, regardless of her feelings toward him something had been bothering her. Why else would she have made those absurd comments about not being attractive? At least her innate good sense had prevailed in rejecting that presumptuous clerk. The pup was no match for her—in any regard. She deserved . . . more. But why should he care about her affairs? That gave him pause to think. Because they had become friends, and friends cared for the happiness of one another. He merely wanted to see her with the chance of being happy. God knows, she deserved that, after all she had been through.

Another ghost of a smile came to his lips when he thought about her parting words to him. The minx, to throw his own set-down back in his face! Throughout all the trying circumstances of her upbringing she had not lost her sharp wit and quick sense of humor. Why, she was the only person besides Henry and Cecelia that he looked forward to conversing with. He would miss that, he supposed, if she married some dull dog like Duckleigh. A dull dog who had the temerity to call her by her given name.

Alex.

He liked the way it sounded on his own tongue. It would be nice to call her that.

He looked up in surprise to see he was already close to his town house. Far from settling his thoughts, the walk had only kept his emotions on edge. It was a novel experience, not having them under rigid control. He found himself feeling the need of something—perhaps a large snifter of warming brandy.

Or perhaps a warm bed. He realized with a start that he hadn't been with a woman since, well, since he had met Miss Chilton. Mayhap that was why he was feeling so agitated. He couldn't remember the last time he had gone so long without the pleasures of a female companion to warm his nights. And yet, though he would have welcomed the physical release, he had not the slightest desire to visit Lady Cameron, or any other lady for that matter. What was the world coming to?

He sighed, perplexed with himself.

A glass of brandy would have to do.

Hammerton paced back and forth over the expensive Oriental carpet in his oak-paneled library, his eyes narrowed in anger. He lashed out in frustration with a booted foot, sending a delicate Louis XIV side table crashing to the floor and the contents of a crystal decanter splashing over the rich brocade of a neighboring settee. Things were not going as he had planned. The Chilton pup was presenting no problem—he still suspected nothing. It was the damned sister who was proving too clever by half. Who could have imagined that a mere female would pose a problem?

At that thought, his teeth bared in a semblance of a smile. How absurd. He relaxed slightly. The notion of being worried about matching wits with a dowdy, on-the-shelf country miss showed how tightly wound he had let himself become. Perhaps Arthur had a point. It was best to finish things off quickly, especially given his cousin's unsteady frame of mind. But Arthur he could handle later.

He glared into the flames of the fire. It was the girl he had to deal with right away, before she nosed any further into the matter. Investigate, indeed. What a ridiculous idea. But she could cause complications. It wouldn't do to have people begin to ask questions about the so-called accidents. He began pacing again, slowly and deliberately as he fell into deep thought. As he turned, his boot came in contact with the fallen decanter and he kicked it aside, shattering the faceted glass. He smirked in satisfaction at the scattered shards. If the meddlesome chit wanted to get to the bottom of things, he would be only too happy to oblige her.

Only it would be the bottom of a river or a ditch.

His hand came up to stroke his jaw. Staring at the broken glass, he was beginning to put together the pieces of a new plan. Yes, he smiled to himself, it would work quite nicely—why, it was even more ingenious than any of the others. Not only would it take care of his immediate problem, it would throw that arrogant Earl of Branford in such disgrace, no respectable person would dare be seen in his presence. He rubbed his hands together in relish at the very thought of it. No question, it was brilliant.

The clock on the mantel chimed the hour. It was only midnight. Why, he could begin putting the plan in motion right away—the man he needed to see was no doubt just beginning to roust himself for his usual activities. Hammerton hurried from the room and barked an order for his carriage to be brought around immediately.

Two nights later, at precisely the same hour, he waited impatiently inside a seedy little pub off a small alleyway in the East End. Though there was precious little chance of being recognized, Hammerton kept the collar of his greatcoat thrown up to shield his face and his hat pulled down low over his brow despite the fetid closeness of the dimly lit room. Finally, a slight man whose pointed features brought to mind those of a weasel sidled in through the smoky haze and slid into the chair opposite the earl. The new arrival darted furtive glances all around before pulling his own worn coat up around his ears.

"Do you have it?" demanded Hammerton.

"Aren't ye gonna offer me summfink to wet me whistle wid?" whined the other man. His grimy hand came up to scratch at the side of his nose. "Yea, 'corse I got it. I's a professional, isn't I?"

Hammerton got up and returned with a full bottle and a single glass.

"Weren't no trouble, t'all, gis like ye said," he went on. "They leaves the back door open, like. A baby could rob 'em blind. Not that there's much worth taking."

Hammerton's eyes narrowed as he watched the fellow take a noisy slurp from the tumbler of gin he'd just helped himself to. "I trust you remembered what I said. I want no appearance of anyone having entered the house."

The man wiped his mouth on his sleeve. "I follow me orders. You know that." He pulled some folded sheets of paper from his pocket. "These are wot yer after, right? Woot ye didn't tell me was that there 'ud be so many bleeding pieces of paper wid writing on 'em. Bloody lucky fer ye that I kin read—I hope ye remembers that in my reward. Took me fer-ever ta find what ye asked fer."

Hammerton glanced over the pages with a look of mounting satisfaction. "These will do."

He pushed a leather purse toward the man. It disappeared from the sticky tabletop with astonishing speed. The second round of gin was finished nearly as fast.

Hammerton was gone before the glass hit the table.

Alex straightened the folds of her gown as her aunt's maid finished arranging her hair, suddenly wishing she had something of a finer silk, cut a little more elegantly, perhaps even showing a bit of . . .

She caught herself and her mouth quirked in a self-deprecating smile. Why, she was in danger of becoming the type of flighty female she abhorred, caring only how her hair was coiffed or whether her gowns were à la mode. She would be well glad when the Season was over and they could return to the country and her comfortable routine. Then she could throw herself into her work undisturbed, with none of the recent distractions of Society.

Or would life seem sadly flat without the stimulation of the new friends she had made? She truly enjoyed the camaraderie and conversations with the other members of the Botanical Society. She could, of course, continue to correspond with them, but it would not be quite the same. And if she were truly honest with herself, she would miss the company of someone else. She had come to look forward to their verbal sparrings, to seeing the glint of understanding in his eyes in reaction to her observations rather than the usual blank or outraged expression. The fact that he never seemed shocked by her opinions or dismissed them out of hand because she was a female was something she would no doubt miss.

She gave a small sigh.

"Is something wrong, Miss Alex?" Her aunt's maid deftly twisted her hair into an artful mass of curls at the nape of her neck, then picked out a few ringlets to frame her face. "You look lovely tonight, if I say so myself."

Even Alex had to admit the effect looked rather well—perhaps her hair wasn't quite as mousy or her eyes as unremarkable as she thought. But she was no match for the likes of voluptuous blondes or the other beautiful, socially polished ladies that Lord Branford obviously spent his nights with.

"Thank you, Maggie," she replied absently. But her real thoughts were on how ridiculous she was being to dwell on the earl. As he himself had made perfectly clear, his affairs were none of her business. Most likely he sought out her conversation merely to relieve his boredom during the tedious balls and routs until it was time for . . . other activities. He certainly never gave any indication that he thought about her in any other light.

Alex looked squarely in the mirror. She saw the sensible, practical person she had always seen. With another sigh, she cautioned herself not to suddenly fall prey to strong emotions—it would only lead to trouble.

A slight frown then creased her lips. In fact, she had no idea why she had become so peevish a few nights ago just because some attractive lady had flirted with Branford. If the gossips were to be believed, that sort of thing happened with astonishing frequency. Of course she paid little attention to wagging tongues, but it was rather amusing to keep up on all the latest *on-dits*. In any case, it was eminently clear that dwelling on the earl was dangerous to her equilibrium.

She was determined to put the gentleman out of her thoughts.

Maggie finished with the last of the pins and stepped back to admire her handiwork. Alex fought back the temptation to pull them all out, put on her spattered smock, and retreat to the safety of her palette and paints. If only it could be that easy. She rose and, after thanking the older woman for her efforts, went downstairs.

Lady Beckworth smiled as Alex looked into the drawing room. "I'm so grateful that you don't mind attending Lady Hopkinton's rout without me, and that the Simpsons are able to take you along with them. You know how dreadfully put out she would be if neither of us put in an appearance. I promise you, I should never hear the end of it."

"Do not trouble yourself," replied Alex. "Though I admit I would much rather spend the evening at home with my work, I shall endeavor to soothe the Lady Hopkinton's feelings with profound expressions of regret from you."

Lady Beckworth muffled an unladylike snort. "Oh dear, that is a scene I should very much like to witness. Do try to be tactful, my dear."

Alex grinned, "She couldn't recognize sarcasm if I brushed it on with linseed oil. But never fear, I *can* be civilized if I apply myself." She reached down to plump the pillow behind her aunt's head. "I've given Cook a new recipe for an herb tisane that I came upon in one of Papa's books. It should help ease your sore throat and allow you to sleep through the night. And don't wait up for me. You need your rest."

"Shall Justin put in an appearance?"

"He doubts he will be free. Apparently he and Charles are engaged to escort Charles's cousins to the theater. But don't fret about me. Mr. Simpson and his wife have assured me that it is of no inconvenience to bring me home as well. You may tell Givens to retire at a decent hour. I will let myself in by the scullery door, just as Justin does."

Lady Beckworth patted Alex's arm. "Do try to have a good time."

"Oh, I shall. But I'm sure it will be a most uneventful evening."

Chapter Six

Arthur Standish looked up from reading the small, flowing script covering a single sheet of cream-colored stationery. He looked puzzled.

"Wherever did you manage to get this? I don't understand . . ."

Hammerton took the paper carefully by one of the corners and slid it back into the drawer of his desk for the moment. "It doesn't signify where I got it. The person is a master at what he does. What matters is that even Miss Chilton would be hard-pressed to say whether she had indeed penned it herself—I assure you, the handwriting and signature are perfect."

The explanation didn't entirely banish the look of confusion from Standish's face and Hammerton had to rein in his mounting impatience. His cousin really was inordinately slow-witted not to realize what was being planned. Thank God he did not have to depend on him for anything other than blind obedience.

His fingers drummed on the polished wood. "I will explain it fully in due time. But right now, we have other things to get in readiness. By the end of the evening, our problems with Miss Chilton will be over."

There were at least some familiar faces in the crowded, overheated room. Though as capacious as any ballroom in

London, the space felt cramped and confining due to Lady Hopkinton's sad lack of taste. The flowers were too garish and overpowering, filling the air with a cloying scent that only accentuated the heaviness of the thick damask drapes that blocked every window.

The music seemed overloud as well, and Alex was grateful when Lady Cecelia Ashton asked if she would like to join her in fetching a glass of ratafia punch in one of the less crowded side rooms. They became engaged in a long conversation over the merits of a certain garden designer, and Alex was pleasantly surprised at how knowledgeable the diminutive lady was, as well as how pithy some of her comments were. And when the talk shifted to life in London and she ventured a few of her own frank opinions on the silliness of certain reigning ideas, it was more than gratifying to see a spark of understanding and amusement in the other woman's eyes. Why, thought Alex, here was one lady of the *ton* with whom she could imagine forming a real friendship.

There was a brief lull as Lady Ashton selected a small plate of biscuits. When she spoke again, the subject was changed once more. "You know, Sebastian told me he greatly enjoyed his visit to Kew Gardens with you."

Alex made a small choking sound on her punch when she realized just who Lady Ashton was referring to.

"He did?" she managed to reply, hoping that the heat she felt stealing over her was not causing her face to flame.

"Yes. In fact, I haven't seen him capable of enjoying himself so since—well, since before Jeremy was killed on the Peninsula. I take it you have heard of that?"

Alex nodded.

Lady Ashton's eyes narrowed. "Vicious rumors," she said quietly. "He affects to pay them no heed, but I know that inside . . . He cared for Jeremy very much . . ." She let her voice trail off, an angry look darkening her porcelain features.

Alex liked her even more for it.

"In any case," continued Lady Ashton. "I think we have you to thank for the change. He is a dear friend—"

Alex stiffened slightly.

"Oh, not that," assured Lady Ashton with a knowing smile. "I am quite happy with my own husband. He and Sebastian have been close friends for an age."

Alex once again felt quite flustered. "I—I can't imagine I have any influence over Lord Branford's moods."

Lady Ashton regarded her shrewdly but remained silent. Alex felt her face flame even more under the scrutiny. She was saved from having to say anything further by the arrival of Lord Ashton.

"My dear," he said, taking his wife firmly by the arm, "your great-aunt has sent me to fetch you to pay your respects—now! I know you have been avoiding her all evening." He turned to smile at Alex. "I beg you will excuse us, Miss Chilton, but I am afraid that family duties call."

"The old dragon calls, you mean," said Lady Ashton under her breath. She gave Alex a parting smile. "I look forward to meeting with you again, Miss Chilton. It has been a most interesting talk."

Alex was more than grateful for the interruption. She most definitely did not want the conversation turning to Lord Branford, of all people, tonight. On that topic her feelings were not those she cared to discuss with anyone. How could she, when she wasn't even sure herself what they were?

Drat the man!

But she had promised to put him out of her mind tonight and she meant to do just that.

She made her way back to the ballroom and headed toward a spot where she had last seen Mr. Simpson and some others of her acquaintance conversing. The dialog there would no doubt be a trifle more heated, but much less inflammatory to her own overwrought emotions.

A liveried footman approached her, a silver tray full of champagne flutes balanced on one hand.

"Miss Chilton?" he asked softly, as he stopped and offered her a glass.

"Yes?" Alex was mystified as to how he knew who she was.

"A gentleman asked that I give you this, but said it was important that no one see," he said in a low voice as he discreetly pressed a note into her gloved hand along with the champagne. "He said to be very careful of what you do from here." With that, he melted back into the crowd.

Alex stood motionless for a moment, then, with feigned nonchalance, strolled to a quiet nook, put down the glass, and took a seat on a small settee, half hidden by a potted ficus tree. Placing her hands in her lap to hide the trembling of her fingers, she unfolded the note and quickly scanned its contents.

If you wish to know the reason for the attacks on your brother, leave at once and take a hansom cab to St. Giles Lane. Turn left, and walk down to the river. I dare not say more or contact you again. Do not delay—his fate is in your hands.

There was no signature.

Alex's face paled. She stuffed the paper into her glove and stood up, her mind racing. She beckoned to another servant serving champagne and sent him toward Mr. Simpson with instructions to inform him that she was returning home early with an indisposition and would not need a ride. Then, with a quick glance left and right, she slipped out of the main room. Her exit didn't attract the least attention and she hurried down a long corridor, past the ladies' withdrawing room, to where a side staircase led down to the main entrance of the town house. It was highly unlikely, she thought, that Lady Hopkinton or any of the guests would even notice she had departed early.

A cold mist rose up from the river, obscuring the sooty brick warehouses and splintered docks in swirling tendrils of fog. Sounds were muffled in the dampness—the creaking of the timbers in the ebbing tide, the lapping of the brackish water against the embankment and the pacing of booted feet on a dirt path.

"What time is it?" Standish halted by the side of a carriage, which had been temporarily stripped of all distinguishing crests. The horses snorted and whisked their tails in response to the creeping chillness in the air. He pulled the thick black scarf wound around his face even higher, so that only the eyes were visible, and peered into the unlit interior.

"Precisely five minutes later than when you last inquired," came a voice from the impenetrable darkness. "She will not be here for at least another hour. I suggest you climb inside before you exhaust yourself with such a pointless display of nerves."

Standish swore under his breath. With one last, jerky look around at the swirls of gray and the overcast sky he got in and threw himself onto the seat opposite his cousin. A spot of orange glowed for a moment, then was followed by a cloud of smoke, thicker and more choking than the air outside. Standish coughed and waved his hand several times in front of his nose to punctuate his distaste. Hammerton ignored him and continued to puff away in a nonchalant manner.

Standish began toying with the pistol in his hand. "It's one thing to deal with another man. I do not fancy the idea of having to shoot a female."

"Yes, your standards are so very high," mocked Hammerton. "Pray, don't waste such sentiments on me. I know you too well. And the plan does not involve putting a bullet into her. The weapons are merely a precaution against the unexpected. As you have noticed, I think ahead. That is why my plans succeed."

"When are you going to tell me the plan?" he demanded in a sulky voice.

The tip of the cigar came alight again as Hammerton drew in a mouthful of the pungent tobacco, then let it out slowly, savoring the taste.

"So you still haven't figured it out?" he asked, a touch of disdain in his voice. "I would have thought the letter I showed you would have made everything exceedingly easy to comprehend."

Standish grunted something unintelligible.

Hammerton heaved a mock sigh. "Ah, well, then let me explain it clearly. As you read, the letter reveals a despondent Miss Chilton, who, having been seduced and abandoned by Lord Branford, finds she can no longer live with her shame and the disgrace she will bring to her family—"

"But Branford has withdrawn from the bet," interrupted Standish. "How are you going to get her to . . ." He suddenly fell silent as his mind began to comprehend the implications of his cousin's words.

"It is finally beginning to dawn on you, is it?"

Standish muttered something through the thick material covering the front of his mouth.

"It won't be dangerous at all. In fact it should be frighteningly simple. She will approach us. I will go to meet her, a single figure bent low, beckoning her to come closer to hear the information she so desperately seeks. You will come up behind her and knock her unconscious with your cosh—what could be easier?

"We'll put her in the carriage and drive along the river until we are close to the neighborhood where the ball took place, within easy walking distance for a young lady. Then the body goes into the water. And it's done. With no possible connection to us. A street urchin will be dispatched with the letter to her aunt's house. And I have taken care to have the hackney driver who will be waiting to pick her up later this evening ready to step forward and swear he saw her walking toward the river, agitated and alone—he will be able to describe her exactly."

He smiled into the darkness. "Poor, dear departed Miss Chilton. Another victim of the Icy Earl. Think you that Society will have anything to do with him after that? He may even be forced to leave the country."

Standish let out a low whistle of admiration. "By God, it is brilliant."

"What did you expect, cousin?" said Hammerton in a self-satisfied tone as he tapped the ashes onto the floor. "What did you expect?"

Standish's eyes mirrored the same smug expression. Then after a moment, they narrowed in concern. "What if she doesn't come?"

Hammerton's eyes fell half-closed as he exhaled another cloud. "Oh, she will come. All we have to do is wait. Our little pigeon will fly straight to us."

Damnation, swore Branford to himself. What the devil was she up to now? He had arrived late, but just in time for his sharp eye to catch the exchange between the waiter and

Alex. Surely she wasn't planning anything as buffleheaded as an elopement with that pup Duckleigh. His teeth set on edge. Of all the idiotic—

But then it struck him that her face had gone white and the look on it as she had slipped from the room was not one of girlish enrapture but rather of grave concern. He let out an exasperated sigh and left the room as well.

She was not difficult to follow. Though she had thrown the hood of her cape up to shield her face, she looked back nary once as she hurried through the clusters of waiting carriages. Branford watched as she signaled to a hansom cab loitering on the street corner ahead, then turned and quickly made his way to where his own coach was drawn to a halt near the end of the line.

"That hackney just pulling away from up there"—he spoke in a low voice to his coachman, so that no inquisitive ears could overhear—"follow it. Discreetly, but on no account are you to lose it."

The man nodded alertly, his mouth set in a hard line that indicated he understood his master's tone. As soon as Branford had climbed in, he maneuvered the horses around the crush of other vehicles and set them off at a smart pace. It proved no problem to quickly fall in behind the lumbering vehicle.

Branford grew crosser and crosser as the hackney passed through the elegant streets of Mayfair into the darkness of less fashionable neighborhoods. A swirling fog crept over the grimy buildings and a dampness in the air told him they were coming closer to the river. On more than one occasion, his man was forced to slow to a walk to avoid coming too close to the other carriage.

An oath escaped his lips. What could the headstrong girl be up to in this neighborhood, at this hour—

His carriage lurched to a sudden halt.

"My lord," hissed his driver.

Branford opened the trap with the tip of his cane.

"The hackney has stopped ahead, sir, and the . . . person appears to be getting out."

Branford moved quickly to open the door, pausing a moment to take the pistol hanging inside and place it in his greatcoat pocket. His boots hit the cobblestones with surprising lightness.

"Wait around the corner," he ordered, then disappeared with a catlike stealth into the swirling mist.

Her figure ghosted in and out of the shadows, forcing him to draw nearer than he would have liked in order not to lose her down some narrow alley. But she headed not into the warren of passageways among the dilapidated warehouses but straight toward the embankment.

A breeze from off the water blew away the fog. Branford pressed up close against a grimy brick wall to avoid being seen. Ahead of Alex, a figure was revealed near the steps leading down to the river. Then his trained eye caught the slight movement of another person, a short distance from the first, trying to remain hidden in the shadows. As the second one turned toward the sound of the approaching footsteps, a glint of steel flashed in the pale moonlight.

"Alex! Get down!" Branford sprang from the wall, racing toward her with long, loping strides as he tore the pistol from his coat.

Alex froze in confusion.

A shot rang out and she crumpled to the ground.

Branford reached her only seconds later. Another bullet whistled past his ear as he crouched over to shield her body with his own. The fog closed in once again, causing him to curse in frustration as he pointed his own weapon toward the impenetrable mist. The instincts of a soldier took over. They knew where he was—he must change that.

He bent lower, gently turning her over to face him. Alex's eyes fluttered open, still a bit dazed.

"Where are you hurt?" he demanded.

"My shoulder. Feels like a bee sting . . ."

His fingers probed at the torn fabric.

"Ouch!"

He grunted something unintelligible, then grasped her around the waist and half dragged her to the shelter of the buildings.

"Can you manage to walk?" he asked, his eyes sweeping the darkness for any sign of movement.

"Of course I can," she answered indignantly. "I'm not—"

"Then do so. Quickly!"

He set her out in front of him and hurried her out of the maze of alleys to where his carriage was waiting. None too gently, he thrust her inside. Then with a last, grim look around he climbed in after her and rapped a signal to his coachman. The horses set off at a gallop.

Alex drew in several deep breaths and closed her eyes. Her mind was reeling with questions, but suddenly she felt very tired and her shoulder began to ache abominably. Unconsciously, she slumped sideways until she came in contact with something very solid and reassuringly warm. A slight shiver ran through her as she lay her head on Branford's shoulder. He shifted slightly and shrugged out of his greatcoat, then she felt the heavy wool enveloping her as he tucked it around her and pulled her close. With a small sigh, she relaxed against him, vaguely aware of an arm circling her waist. Then everything became very hazy.

The next thing Alex was aware of, Branford was drawing his coat tighter around her and guiding her down from the carriage and through a side door.

"Where are—"

He cut off her question by dropping the coat to the floor

and sweeping her up into his arms. As he strode down the hallway they met his butler, who held a candle aloft in order to investigate the noise.

"Hot water and bandages in my chamber. Immediately!" shouted Branford as he went up the massive carved stairs two at a time.

Flinging open a heavy oaken door, he crossed the thick carpet, put her down on an immense four-poster bed, and turned to light a branch of candles.

"My lord, you have brought me to . . ."

"To my town house, Miss Chilton. I can hardly deposit you on your aunt's doorstep until I have ascertained the extent of your injury."

Alex sat up rather abruptly. "I assure you, sir, it is nothing more than a scratch. You needn't . . ."

His fingers were already at the neck of her gown. She shivered slightly as he undid a few of the buttons and gently slid the material down to bare her shoulder. There was a discreet knock on the door.

"Enter, Hopkins."

The butler came in with a basin and a length of linen on a tray. Branford motioned toward a small table by the bed.

"You may put it there. I shan't need you any more tonight."

If the man experienced any surprise at finding a young lady with a bullet wound in his master's bedchamber in the middle of the night, he betrayed no sign of it. He merely bowed slightly.

"Good night, then, m'lord."

Branford moistened a soft cloth and carefully sponged at the gash in her shoulder. She was amazed at how gentle his touch was, how deft the movements of his strong hands.

"You are lucky, Miss Chilton," he murmured as he tore a long strip from the length of linen. "The wound is not deep and if you take care, there should be no need to consult a physician."

"I am quite knowledgeable about herbs as well, sir, and know how to make a salve to aid healing. There is no need for concern."

He finished bandaging her shoulder in silence. Then he grasped her other shoulder and turned her to face him.

"No need for concern," he repeated in a low voice. Alex was so close to him she could almost feel the heat from his blazing eyes. "Then perhaps you can explain to me how a supposedly rational being could act in such an addlepated, cork-brained, idiotic manner. Are you truly daft, Miss Chilton, or merely as foolish as the worst of your sex are wont to be?"

Alex was taken aback by the real anger in his voice.

"I received a note concerning Justin. I was following the instructions . . ." She faltered, realizing how lame it sounded, even to her own ears.

"I see," he interrupted. "So it is your habit of blindly following even the most patently absurd directions, in your arrogant assumption that you can handle any situation that arises. I hadn't thought you so stupid."

Alex's eyes flared with her own hot anger. "What would you have me do?" she demanded. "Stand by and see my brother murdered?" She was dangerously close to yelling.

"He is no longer a child, Alex. Let him be a man and deal with it himself."

In the heat of the argument neither of them seemed to notice his use of her given name.

"Oh, you think me a managing female," she sputtered. "How dare you, sir! You know nothing—besides, he refuses to acknowledge any danger. He thinks I am imagining it. Well, do you think tonight is a bad dream?"

"Indeed I do," he muttered through clenched teeth. In a louder voice he added, "Then you might have come to me."

Her chin drew up imperceptibly. For some inexplicable reason, an image of Lady Cameron floated across her mind. Blond. Beautiful. Beckoning. "Don't be ridiculous," she said roughly. "What possible reason have you to care about me and my family?"

It was his turn to feel stung by her words. "I have little choice when I observe a lone female of my acquaintance skulking off in the dead of night. Though you may not countenance it, I have *some* sense of honor!"

His hand was still gripping her good shoulder and as he spoke, the other one came up to the bandaged one. Without thinking, he began shaking her. "If you *ever* do anything so idiotic again, I swear I shall—"

Alex snapped. He was hurting her, both with his grip and the truth of his words. Her hand shot out and delivered a resounding slap across his face.

Both of them were rendered speechless for a moment. Alex's mouth dropped in belated shock at what she had done. An unreadable emotion flashed in Branford's eyes. He opened his mouth as if to say something.

Instead, his lips came down on hers, not tentatively, but hard and demanding. Alex stiffened in utter surprise, then found herself responding with equal passion. Her arms flung up around his neck, her fingers reveling in the silky feel of the long, dark locks that curled against his collar. She felt herself crushed to his chest, felt the heat of his skin, the pounding of his pulse which echoed her own racing heart.

She had never imagined a kiss could be like this. On one or two other occasions in the past she had allowed a gentleman's lips to brush hers. But this was so much more . . . intimate. His tongue urged her mouth to part and the feel of him touching her in such a way sent a surge of fire rushing through her body. Hesitantly her own tongue met his and she gave a low moan as she tasted the exotic spiciness of his mouth.

At the sound, he deepened the kiss with an intensity that took her breath away. Then he broke it off to run his lips with gossamer lightness over her cheekbones, then down the inside curve of her throat.

"Don't ever scare me again like that, Alex," he murmured between caresses.

All at once, all the reason, all the common sense, all the practicality that had dominated her life to that point deserted her. She knew, beyond all doubt, that regardless of the consequences she must seize the moment.

"Sebastian," she whispered. "Make love to me."

His eyes glittered a deeper blue than she had ever seen as they searched her face. "Alex, I . . ."

"Please." Perhaps it was very wrong, but she couldn't help herself. The need for him was overwhelming. Her hand slipped tentatively inside his shirt, her fingers seeking out the bare skin.

His hands tenderly brushed the tendrils near her face. She was trusting him with her honor, and the thought was overwhelming. Why, he felt almost dizzy with a rush of emotion. In that moment he made the decision, for he suddenly realized what she meant to him, to his future.

There was no reason to turn back—she would be his in name as well as spirit soon enough.

With a deep groan he wrenched at the folds of his neckcloth, tearing it off and throwing the length of linen to the floor. Then he yanked at the fastenings of his shirt, sending the buttons flying and exposing himself to the waist. Alex ran her palms over the taut muscles and flat planes of his torso, her eyes wide with wonderment.

"You are beautiful beyond imagination," she whispered as she brushed the dark curls on his chest. Looking up at him, a shy smile came to her lips.

The rigid control that usually governed his features was suddenly gone, replaced by a look of need as urgent as her own. He slipped the bodice of her dress down to her waist, then eased her chemise off her shoulders as well. His hands cupped her firm, rounded breasts, the thumbs gently coaxing the nipples to immediate response.

"You are as lovely, as luminous as one of your exquisite paintings," he said softly.

Whatever words she was about to say caught in her throat as he lowered his head and took the delicate flesh in his mouth.

She cried out in amazed pleasure.

Branford made a low sound from deep in his throat as he threw back the covers of the bed. He rapidly removed the rest of her garments until she lay totally unclothed on the snowy sheets. His ruined shirt was tossed over a chair, then his boots came off one by one and clattered to the floor. He turned away from her to unfasten the buttons on his breeches and stripped them off over his powerful thighs. When he faced her in the flickering candlelight he, too, was naked, and fully aroused.

She stared at him in wonder. He radiated strength and a rampant masculinity. Having lived all her life in the country, she knew something of the physical act, but looking at his manhood jutting forward from the dark curls she gave a nervous swallow.

"I am aware of what is about to happen next, but I think, that is, I fear—we may not fit."

Branford gave a husky chuckle as he climbed onto the bed and straddled her willowy form. "You may trust me, little one. We shall fit quite nicely." His expression turned serious. "If you are afraid, or are having second thoughts you have only to say so." His mouth quirked at the corners. "It may be the death of me, but God help me, I shall take you home . . ."

She reached up and pulled his head down to hers.

The kiss was gentler this time, unrushed but no less passionate. As their lips played together, his knee came between her thighs, slowly easing them open. His fingers trailed down over her stomach, then brushed through her own downy curls and touched her most intimately.

Alex gave another soft cry at the exquisite jolt of fire that his touch sent through her body. She arched up to meet his hand, wondering at the novel sensation of dampness between her legs.

"You are sweetly ready for me," he whispered as he slid his finger inside her.

Her nails dug into his shoulders as her narrow passage adjusted to the fit. Slowly, he began moving it in and out. Her body, tight with pleasure, moved instinctively to match his rhythm.

"Good Lord," he groaned. "I feel like a callow schoolboy about to spill my seed here and now—Alex, I can wait no longer!"

His hand came away.

"Sebastian! Don't stop," she cried softly.

His voice was taut with emotion. "My sweet, the devil himself could not drag me away now."

He lowered himself, thrusting his rigid manhood gently into her. His own sound of pleasure echoed in the room as her honeyed passage closed tightly around him. The feel of it nearly sent him over the edge. He fought to regain control, then pushed ahead slowly until he felt the barrier of her maidenhood. Withdrawing slightly, he pressed forward again, then again.

Alex flinched slightly.

He became still. "Did I hurt you?" he asked, his voice full of concern.

"Only for a moment, and it is past. Now it feels . . . wonderful."

Her hips rose, burying him deep within her. With a muffled groan, he brought her legs around his hips and began to move to the music of his passion.

Alex was responding to the same glorious rhythm. Her breath was coming in rapid gulps. Each of Branford's thrusts was building a shuddering, delicious tension throughout her whole being that somehow she knew must be released, though she knew not how. Her hands roamed over the rippling muscles of his back as if seeking the answer there, and her hips rose and fell with his tempo. Sensing the burning need building within her, his pace quickened.

She arched one more time and suddenly was aware of nothing but a surging wave coursing out from the center of her being. His name burst from her lips as she sought to merge herself more fully with him. Her hands grasped at his buttocks, urging him deeper. His own hoarse cry joined hers as he buried himself to the hilt and poured his life-giving essence into her.

The room was utterly silent save for their ragged breathing. With his full weight pressing against her, Alex felt the melding of their beating hearts. Her own body felt oddly unreal, as if she couldn't move a muscle if her life depended on it. She sensed that all the tension had drained from Branford as well, all the hard edges gone and a strange vulnerability about him. He was still inside her, and as she caressed his heated skin, she found herself wishing she could stay a part of him, help him fight off whatever demons caused him to erect such careful defenses around his feelings.

With a deep sigh, he rolled to one side and settled her head on his chest. It was damp and the scent of his exertion made her feel almost giddy. His hand ran through her loosened tresses, which tumbled down over her shoulders onto the sheets.

"Tis like spun silk," he murmured.

"It's mousy," she sighed.

He smiled. "For an artist, you are remarkably unobservant. It is a rich burnt umber, with highlights of sienna." He held a strand up to the candlelight. "And perhaps a touch of cinnabar with—"

"My lord, how do you know the palette so well?"

Branford's eyebrows rose in mock consternation. "My lord, is it then? A moment ago it was Sebastian."

Alex felt a slight flush steal over her at the thought of her unbridled physical response to him.

"Say it again." His voice was rough with emotion though it was no louder than a whisper.

"Sebastian," she said, looking up into his sapphire eyes.

"Again!"

She said it once more, slowly savoring the sound of each letter.

His lips came down on hers—hard, possessively—then he blew out the candles.

Alex had no idea how long she had been asleep. In fact, as she was roused by a gentle shake, it took her a moment to realize it was not all some exotic dream. That was made abundantly clear as her hand stirred over flesh that was definitely not her own. The flat, muscular planes of the stomach. Skin roughened with hair and—

"Oh!" She sat up.

Branford tightened his arm around her waist and pulled her back down to the sheets.

"Careful with your sweet caresses, little one, else you will have me starting again," he teased.

Alex's eyes widened in surprise. "It can be . . . done more than once in a night?"

He gave a throaty chuckle. "Tis a pity I cannot give my scientist empirical proof. But you must return home. It is already later than I wish."

She sighed. "Must I?"

He pressed a kiss on her hair, then reached up to relight the candles. "I am afraid so. Can you manage to dress without assistance?"

"I am not some fine lady—I'm quite used to dressing myself."

An unreadable look flashed across his features. "Make haste if you will, then, while I arrange for the carriage." He swung his long legs off the bed and retrieved his breeches and boots. He tugged them on quickly and fetched an undamaged shirt from the stately dresser to the side of the four-poster.

"Ten minutes?" He was at the door.

She nodded, acutely aware that the sheet had pulled away to expose one of her breasts and one willowy leg. She found herself wishing she were smaller, rounder, somehow more ladylike.

His eyes lingered on her for an instant, then he turned abruptly and was gone.

A short while later, Alex slanted a sideways glance at Branford as the carriage made its way through the darkened streets. He seemed lost in thought, his brow slightly furrowed as he stared, unseeing, at the curtained window. She felt a knot form in the pit of her stomach. Was he regretting the whole evening? Why, she had as good as thrown herself at him. Men, she had heard, had different . . . needs. Had she fanned some fire he had wished to leave unlit? Or worse, had he formed a disgust of her, thinking her no better than a— Dear God! A tremor ran through her and she shrank back into the leather seat.

"Are you chilled?" he asked softly.

These were the first words he had spoken since they had entered the carriage.

She shook her head, not trusting her voice to mask her anxiety.

He gave a faint smile but made no move to bridge the gap between them. No comforting shoulder to lean on this time, no solid warmth from the feel of his arm around her waist.

The carriage pulled to a halt. Branford alighted and helped her down. They were in a side street, far enough away from the flickering streetlight that they would appear as mere shadows to anyone passing by.

"You are sure you need no accompaniment—"

"As you have said, the less risk of being observed, the better. I can manage quite well."

"Your shoulder—"

She waved him silent. "It is not a matter for concern. As you saw yourself, it is hardly more than a scratch." She took a deep breath. "Thank you for your . . . assistance tonight." She was aware of how painfully stilted the words sounded, but she was too confused to know what else to say or do. "Good night"—she paused slightly, then added—"my lord."

"Good night, Miss Chilton."

She looked as if to say something more, then turned quickly and passed through a small side gate. He watched her cross a narrow garden and disappear into the back of the house. Letting out a ragged sigh, he climbed back into the carriage.

Branford pressed his head back against the squabs. What was happening to his vaunted self-control? He hadn't meant for things to turn out as they did. But when she had looked at him with such frank need, why, he couldn't keep his own desire in check. And her response to him! His groin tightened at the mere thought. She had wanted him. Not his title. Not his fortune. Not the excitement of his reputation. There was something achingly sweet about the way she had looked at his nakedness, had cried out his name as he brought her to climax.

He raked his hand through his hair. He hadn't dared touch her again—nay, he had hardly even dared look at her again—for fear that he wouldn't be able to let her go. Scandal was the last thing he would allow to come down on either of them. Yet it had taken all of his willpower to deliver her back to her aunt's house.

A disturbing thought struck him. She had been so quiet during the ride. Was she regretting her actions? Had he taken advantage of her heightened emotions? Good God, she had narrowly missed death! Perhaps she would have embraced *anyone* to affirm she was alive. His jaw clenched at the idea of her touching any other man the way she had touched him. Not bloody likely! She was his, irrevocably his—though, he smiled ruefully to himself, she might need additional convincing of that.

What did he mean by that? His jaw stayed tight. He wasn't sure he could even admit to himself what his feelings were. Since his cousin's death he had worked so very hard to have none.

Such haunting questions would no doubt plague him for the rest of the night. He let out another sigh, then rapped on the trap and gave orders to proceed to his club. He wasn't ready to face an empty bed, still redolent with the passion of their lovemaking. If he couldn't have the fire of her kisses, he would have to settle for the fire of some strong spirits. Maybe that could douse the fire in his loins.

* * *

"Get hold of yourself," snarled Hammerton as he stalked to the door of the club's deserted reading room and pulled it shut.

Standish's hands were still shaking though he had just downed his second brandy. "How did he know?" There was a note of rising panic in his voice.

"No doubt he followed the chit. Tis a pity your aim is not as good as mine."

Standish poured another glass from the decanter on the side table, sloshing some of it over the polished mahogany surface. Hammerton regarded him with disgust.

"Do you think she's . . . dead?" asked Standish after taking a hurried gulp.

Hammerton shrugged, his lips turning into a bloodless smile. "Impossible to tell. But that would work out just as well—perhaps even better. Branford would have a great deal to explain. A lone female, a deserted part of town—why he might even be tried for murder. Everyone would believe it possible." His eyes closed briefly in contemplation of such an event and the smile became entirely real.

"Why, that's devilishly clever thinking on your part," said Standish slowly. The spirits were finally beginning to take hold and he relaxed enough to break into his own wolfish grin. "No doubt you are right."

"Try not to forget that, Arthur," replied Hammerton. "Trust me. Our plans will not be thwarted." He took the glass from Standish's hand and put it down on the table. "I think it is time you return to your lodgings."

"But I plan to go on to—" whined Standish.

"Not tonight, Arthur," ordered Hammerton. "In your current state, your tongue would no doubt be flapping as wildly as the sheets. We cannot afford such a thing—is that clear? You will retire until you have rein on your emotions."

Standish's eyes flared, but he said no more.

They began to leave the room when the sound of a voice caused Hammerton to grasp his cousin's shoulder and pull him back.

"What did you say?" Branford drew to a halt not ten paces from where the other two men stood shielded by the half-closed door.

"Begging your lordship's pardon, but your man Sykes arrived not ten minutes ago looking for you, sir. Said it was urgent. I put him in the library since he asked to wait," said a nervous servant. "Did I do right, sir?"

Branford's brows came together. "Yes," he replied absently. "Wait here."

Sykes turned from the fire as the earl entered the room.

"Sorry, Cap'n, but I discovered some rather interesting news in East Anglia. Rushed back as fast as I could—hope it ain't too late."

The two of them put their heads together and spoke in low tones for a short while.

"So you see, Cap'n, I thought you should know, seeing as how the man's on his deathbed, like. You were right—"

"Excellent thinking, Sykes," interrupted Branford. "You can tell me all the details in the carriage ride north. Go tell Brown we leave immediately."

Sykes nodded and hurried from the room.

Branford made to follow, then hesitated, a slight frown on his face. After a moment of reflection, he strode over to the writing desk behind the settee and took up a quill and sheet of paper. He hesitated again, pen poised over the blank sheet. Good Lord, how should he address her that was neither too formal nor too—

He took a deep breath. He was too agitated to polish words as nicely as he would have wished. He gave up and quickly slashed a few lines across the paper in his distinctive script:

> *My Dear,*
> *I've been called away on a matter of grave importance. I shall call on you as soon as I am able and hope to have some interesting news for you. In any case, we have much to discuss. In the meantime, be very careful and convince Justin to do the same.*
> *S.*

He read it over, then folded and sealed the note. It was hardly a lover's note, but it would have to do. He forbore to add in writing that the interesting news would also include the acquisition of a special license. That, no doubt, would indeed be a matter of lengthy discussion, given her opinion on the matrimonial state.

The servant hadn't budged. Branford paused and pressed the note into his hand, along with a few gold coins.

"Deliver this to Miss Chilton at 30 Half Moon Street without delay."

"Yes, my lord!"

Branford signaled for his greatcoat and left the club.

Hammerton waited a moment then slithered out to where the servant was still staring at the guineas in his hand, not quite believing his good fortune.

"I happened to hear my good friend the earl request that you deliver a message for him. As it happens, I am passing that way right now on my way home and would be happy to see it safely into the hands of the right person—as a personal favor to his lordship."

The man looked confused. "I don't know, sir—"

"Nonsense." Hammerton plucked the paper from the

man's hand and added another coin to his riches. "Why should you have to venture out in the dead of night when I may be of service to a friend."

The man stared at the coins. "Very well, my lord, if you're sure—"

"Have no fear. I shall take care of the matter."

The note went into Hammerton's pocket.

Chapter Seven

Alex was not in the best of moods. She surveyed the crowded ballroom and realized there wasn't one soul she wished to converse with. Not even the cluster of Botanical Society members hashing over the latest lecture on flora of the East Indies held any particular interest for her tonight.

Men, she thought acidly as she made her way to a small settee screened from general view by an arrangement of potted palms. *Lord knows they were nothing but trouble*. She knew it had been a big mistake letting emotion overcome reason. The trouble was, she fumed, once the proverbial cat was out of the bag, it was awfully difficult to disengage its claws and stuff it back inside.

Her eyes roamed the room once again. He wasn't here tonight either. It was now five days since— Bloody hell.

Her state of mind was not improved by the thought of what else had happened that night. Any doubt that a real threat to her brother's life existed had been shattered by the crack of a bullet—but she still had no clue as to why. Or who.

"Is something wrong? If looks could kill, you'd have done away with half the *ton* tonight."

Alex's head shot up. "It would be no great loss," she muttered as Justin sat down beside her.

He gave her a searching look. "What has you so out of

sorts? You've been in a black mood for the past few days now."

"Nonsense," she replied, a little sharply. "I simply am tiring of the endless rounds of balls and routs and teas and morning visits—I would prefer to be back at home where it is possible to work without all the distractions."

Justin regarded her with pointed concern. "I'm sorry. I know you are tolerating all of this for my sake, but lately I had thought that, well, perhaps you were enjoying yourself as well."

"The Botanical Society is interesting enough," she answered neutrally. "But I have been neglecting my own work."

Justin was silent for a few moments as he appeared to contemplate the intricate patterns formed by the softly swaying fronds.

"Have you seen Lord Branford?" he asked abruptly. "There is a matter I wish to ask his opinion on."

"Has he not been around?" She hoped her voice did not really sound as brittle as it did to her own ear. "I hadn't noticed."

Justin's brows came together a fraction. He opened his mouth as if to speak, then hesitated and let out a deep sigh instead.

"Perhaps you are right. Perhaps we should return home," he said softly. "Things appear hopeless with Anne's father, and Viscount Adderley is beginning to pay particular attention to her. I should just as soon not have to stand around helplessly and be spectator to that."

Alex felt a stab of guilt. Here she was so caught up in her own affairs that she had neglected to see her brother's pain. She slipped her hand over his.

"How selfish of me," she exclaimed. "I've thought of naught but my own petty problems. Come, tell me why you think things are truly so bleak. Surely you don't doubt Anne's feelings . . ."

Hammerton noticed the two siblings buried among the plants, deep in conversation. He was reminded of the note he had intercepted from Branford, and how it revealed a growing intimacy between the earl and the Chiltons that didn't auger well for his plans. In fact, it had been a cause for concern over the past few days. His lips pursed in thought for a few moments, then curled into a bloodless smile. He strolled to where his cousin was laughing over a bawdy joke with a group of young bucks. Throwing his arm casually over Standish's shoulder, he disengaged him from the other gentlemen and steered him toward the back of the ballroom.

"You wish to have Branford removed as an ally of the Chiltons?" whispered Hammerton. "I have an idea. The two of them are alone over there behind the potted palms. Follow my lead and in five minutes they will be more than happy to stick a knife in those elegant ribs."

He brought them to a halt behind the settee where they were hidden from view by another arrangement of trees but close enough that any conversation would be audible to those seated on the other side.

"Nasty business," said Hammerton in a voice dripping with concern. "I find young Chilton a very pleasant fellow, and his sister is charming as well. Someone should warn them of the danger."

Justin made as if to speak, but Alex gestured for him to remain silent.

Standish, for once, followed his cue perfectly. "Surely you exaggerate?"

Hammerton heaved a sigh. "I wish that it were so. To be honest, I would not have thought even such an unprincipled rake as Branford would stoop so low."

"Just what do you mean?"

"Making sport with an innocent."

"No!" Standish feigned shock. "No gentleman—"

"I would not have believed it either if I hadn't witnessed it myself." He lowered his voice just a little. "It's right there in the betting book at the club. Imagine, he actually wagered five hundred pounds that he could—well, to put it bluntly—mount the poor girl."

Alex went cold inside.

"The blackguard!" exclaimed Standish.

"Quite. Deucedly awkward though, to broach such a delicate subject to the young man. Don't quite know the fellow well enough."

"Yes, I see your point."

"Well, I shall try to think of some way to alert him. It would be ungentlemanly to let such behavior go unchecked. I should never forgive myself if the young lady came to any harm." With that, Hammerton motioned for them to move off, a look of malevolent satisfaction spreading over his face.

Alex's nails dug nearly deep enough into her palms to draw blood. There was a dull roaring in her ears and she found herself wondering if, for the first time in her life, she was going to succumb to the utterly ridiculous feminine weakness of fainting on the spot. But she had never been one to wilt in the face of adversity, she reminded herself grimly. Her shock quickly turned to a seething anger. She gritted her teeth and imagined slicing up a certain portion of the earl's magnificent anatomy—inch by inch.

"Alex . . ." Justin's face was white with concern as he searched for words.

"You needn't worry that I'm about to fall into a fit of girlish hysterics." Her voice was under rigid control. "At my advanced age, I have few of the illusions of a young miss and am not so naive as to the ways of the world. If Lord Branford, for whatever reason, wants to play—"

"We don't even know if it is true," pointed out Justin in a near whisper.

Alex compressed her lips as she brushed a lock of hair from her cheek. "I thought it was you who expected the worst from him."

Justin colored. "It's just that now I—I just don't believe he would do such a thing," he said in a near whisper. "Do you?"

Alex didn't answer his question. "You know very well I sought out the earl for my own reasons. I am fully aware of his reputation. If he chooses to amuse himself with his own little games, that is his concern, not mine."

She forced a smile as Justin's eyes bore into her. "Here is Anne looking for you. I expect you are promised for the next set."

"But Alex—"

"Put the whole thing from your mind. That is what I intend to do. Anyway, it isn't as if I have been silly enough to form a tendre for the man—or have imagined he has any such feelings for me." She shrugged. "I think I shall see if Aunt Aurelia is ready to leave, I find the evening has become exceeding dull."

Branford gave a snort of frustration as he folded the sheets of paper and put them back into his pocket. The elder Chilton had been a damned obtuse individual, which made his code that much more difficult to break. And what the deuce were those little symbols that looked like hatchets, or some such thing, interspersed among the random letters? A professional soldier's logic was child's play compared to that of an introverted scientist.

To add to the mystery, the servant hovering on his

deathbed had had the temerity to expire before Branford arrived in East Anglia, leaving him with only fragments of a jumbled story—and an odd one at that. From the account Sykes had given him, the man's mind was already wandering. What was truth and what was mere figments of a dying man's imagination was difficult to discern.

All in all, it had been a waste of nearly a week. He shifted impatiently against the squabs as the carriage rolled past the outskirts of London. Well, not quite a waste, he corrected himself as another sheet of paper crackled in his breast pocket. He had been close enough to Riverton to stop and attend to one other important matter. The local bishop had been more than happy to comply with his request for a special license, handing it over with unctuous wishes for the quick arrival of an heir.

The journey had provided him with many long hours of contemplation. Mental arguments had raged back and forth. In the end, all the careful reasonings and rigid logic were no more than meaningless words. The essence of it all was that his life would be sadly flat—and yes, lonely—without her.

He was tired of living in a carefully constructed shell. The thought of watching her eat toast and jam at breakfast, of seeing her paint-smudged face furrow in concentration as she worked, of sharing laughter and arguments brought a poignant smile to his lips. And the thought of her in his bed every night, looking at him with the sweet hunger he had seen the other night made the heat rise in him. He felt the front of his breeches tighten and realized that in regard to Miss Alexandra Chilton, he had totally lost his vaunted ability to control his emotions.

And yet he was more than willing to lower his defenses to her. She had trusted him from the beginning. Trusted that he was more than the monster painted by the gossips, trusted that he would not hurt her. She had trusted, in fact, her whole self to him. That meant everything to him.

The carriage hit a rut in the road, causing the small bandbox on the seat beside him to jostle his elbow. Another smile lit his face as he contemplated which of his offerings would please Alex more—the marriage license or the rare specimen of *Nopalxocia phyllanthoides*, that he had had the gardener at Riverton dig up for her. He was well aware that she had no high regard for his species in general, but she had also shown that she was not altogether averse to some of its charms. He felt confident he could convince her that they might grow together quite nicely, that his was not a nature that would send out grasping tendrils to strangle or choke down the nearest living thing.

He glanced out the carriage window, impatient to arrive at Lady Beckworth's town house yet oddly nervous as well. How did she seem to reduce him to feeling like an awkward mooncalf rather than the "Icy Earl" that Society regarded with a mixture of awe and fear? He certainly didn't feel either icy or in control at the thought of her. But then again, Alex Chilton had kept him off-balance from the first time he had met her.

Would to heaven it would stay that way.

The elderly butler took Branford's coat and cane with his customary grimace at having to shuffle from a comfortable chair to open the door.

"Miss Alex is working in the library, my lord," he intoned, hunching his shoulders at the thought of having to walk down the hallway.

Branford suppressed a slight smile. "If you don't mind, Givens, I shall announce myself."

With his precious box under his arm, he approached the room with a mounting sense of anticipation.

She was indeed at work. Her features were totally focused

as she bent close to the textured paper on the easel to lay in a delicate wash of color. Branford paused to regard her through the half-opened door—she was so intent on her painting that she hadn't heard his steps. There was a smudge of indeterminate color on her left cheekbone and the tip of her tongue was just visible through lips parted in concentration. The sight of it sent a flash of heat through his body as he thought of the last time they had been together and how it had felt on his bare skin. He realized with a jolt that was almost physical how much he had missed her.

And yet, he was reluctant to intrude, his attention captivated by the nuances of her expression, the deft movement of her graceful hands, the delicacy of her touch. Unaware of being observed, she worked with an inner confidence while he, strangely, felt a certain shyness rooting him in place.

Chiding himself for acting like a mooncalf, he waited until her brush lifted from the paper, then stepped quietly into the room.

"I hope this means my hibiscus is finished."

Alex whirled around at the sound of his voice.

Her face was pinched and there were faint smudges under the eyes, as if her nights had been fitful. Rather than the undisguised warmth that he had become accustomed to in her glance, there was a veiled grayness to her expression. He walked to the table and put the box down.

"What is wrong, Alex?"

He caught a flicker of some emotion at the sound of her given name before she turned away to slowly and deliberately rinse her brush, then wipe it on a clean rag.

"Only that I do not like to be interrupted when I am at work." Her voice was cool, almost harsh. "I believe I have mentioned that before."

He frowned at the sight of her rigid shoulders. "Alex, look at me."

She turned slowly. Her face was composed, only the set of the jaw betraying the underlying tension.

"Don't play me for a fool. It is obvious—"

"Play *you* for a fool," she echoed. "No, sir, rather it is *I* who do not care for the game any longer."

Branford took a step closer to her. "What in the name of heaven are you talking about?" His expression was one of puzzled consternation. He reached out his hand to touch her cheek but she shied away.

Her gaze locked with his and her mouth set in a hard line. "Very well," she said. "Since you seem reluctant to lay things in the open, I shall do it for you. We are both adults after all, so there is little need for prevarication." Her face was a stony mask. "Is it true that you entered a wager in the betting book at your club for five hundred pounds that you could"—she took a breath of air to steady her voice, then went on—"that you could—I believe the term was mount—me?"

Branford's face drained of all color. He was utterly still save for a slight twitch in the muscle of his locked jaw.

"Alex—" he began.

She cut him off sharply. "It is not a difficult question, Lord Branford. Is it true or isn't it? Yes or no."

"Yes." His voice was barely more than a whisper.

Alex bent her head and began to fiddle with her brushes to hide her trembling hands. She chose one whose sable hair tapered to a perfect point, tested its feel, then returned it to the earthenware jar.

"I must fetch my other brushes—I wish to get back to work, if you please. No doubt you are able to find your own way out, just as you found it in."

She made as if to go by him, but this time his hand came to rest on her arm.

"Alex, I never . . ." He hesitated, seeming to struggle for words.

Her mouth set in a tight smile. "Oh come now, you needn't feel you must invent some apology. It isn't necessary. As I said before, we are both adults." She brushed a ringlet of hair from her cheek, adding another tone to the smudge already there. "Anyway, as I intend never to marry, I was curious about the physical act—and why not experience it with someone who is said to be so very skilled at it? After all, you've had such a great deal of practice, haven't you?" Her eyes had become overly bright, brimming with a hurt her words tried to belie. "Now, sir, if you will excuse me." She wrenched her arm free and fled the room, leaving Branford in stunned silence.

He stood motionless, struggling to master his feeling of utter shock. He felt as if he had been pushed from a cliff and was falling, falling into a vast black void.

"Have you a shred of decency left, or do you also intend to break your promise to meet my challenge?"

Branford's eyes closed for a moment, then he turned slowly to meet Justin's burning glare. The young man's face was taut with anger, made fiercer by disillusionment. His hands clenched at his sides were white at the knuckles. As he stood blocking the doorway, he struggled manfully to keep his shoulders from sagging with disappointment.

"What a bloody sapskull I was to believe you actually . . ." He grimaced in self disgust. "Well? Will you show any honor?"

Branford rubbed his eyes wearily. When his hand fell away, the young man was surprised to see a spasm of naked pain evident on the earl's face before his expression became entirely blank.

"Send your second to Ashton. He will arrange things," said Branford in a low, resigned tone. "And for God's sake, man," he added, "choose someone with discretion and a rein on his tongue, else your sister will be fodder for the gossips!"

A short while later, Alex returned to the library, closed the door firmly, and locked it with a twist of the heavy brass key. She undid the strings to a canvas roll and added an assortment of different-sized brushes to those already standing in the crock by her easel. Mechanically her fingers reached for a square-tipped one, dipped it in a glass of clean water, and began mixing a new tint on her palette. It was then that she noticed the small box still sitting on the edge of the oak table. She stared at it for a lengthy time, then put her brush down and slowly walked over to it. After wiping her hands on the sides of her old gown, she lifted the top and stared down at the intricate veined leaves of a small plant, its roots carefully balled in a piece of damp burlap. Her breath caught in her throat with a tiny sound. Sinking into the nearest chair, she buried her head between her arms and let the tears come at last.

"Are you utterly mad!"

Henry Ashton laid aside the papers he had been studying and peeled off his reading spectacles, as if hoping a clearer view of his friend's face would reveal the words he had just heard were nothing more than a bad jest.

"If you do not wish to stand for me I shall go elsewhere, Henry. Do not feel in the least obliged."

"Damnation, you know very well I'd roast in hell rather than betray our friendship in such a manner," he muttered. "Trouble is, Cecelia will no doubt roast *both* of us if she gets wind of this."

Branford gave a tight smile. "Then let us make certain she does not."

Ashton nodded glumly. "Perhaps I can resolve this unfortunate matter with whomever young Chilton sends to me."

The earl's expression became grim. "I think that well night impossible now, Henry." He let out his breath in a heavy sigh. "The pup hasn't a decent gun to his name. Offer the use of this set to his second, if you will." He placed a polished rosewood case on the desk.

Ashton gave a snort of disgust as he opened the lid. "From Mantons, naturally." His eyes narrowed. "Those aren't your regular pair. And those aren't your initials engraved on the butts."

"No, they were meant for him in any case. Al—Miss Chilton had mentioned his birthday was approaching." His mouth twisted into an unwilling smile. "A gentleman should have a decent gun with which to entrust his honor."

"So you are providing him a deadly accurate weapon," he observed with a touch of asperity. "Do you plan to forgo your own ball and powder as well, to make the match more even? I know you, damn it!" His voice began to rise. "I know you damn well won't put a bullet in the pup. What in the devil's name is this all about? Because I also know you would never—"

"Henry," said Branford softly, "kindly keep your voice down."

Ashton's mouth snapped shut.

"And as to my reasons, I will not discuss them. As I said, the choice is entirely yours."

It was Ashton's turn to let out a sigh. "I shall make it for the north clearing at Houndslow Heath. Tomorrow morning, then?"

Branford compressed his lips into a grim smile. "I am acquainted with the spot. I shall see you there at dawn."

The mist swirled in the gray dawn light, nearly obscuring the three figures that stood at the edge of the clearing. Two carriages waited a short distance away, black smudges against the hazy outline of trees. The only sounds were the muffled jangling of the harnesses as the horses shifted in their traces and the restless pacing of one of the figures.

Lord Ashton turned back in the other direction, throwing another wrathful look at the two young men huddled close together. He muttered something unintelligible under his breath then shifted the wooden case that was clamped tightly under one arm.

"Once again, I'll ask you to reconsider this folly. Surely any imagined"—he stressed the word, adding a tinge of sarcasm—"insult can be settled by gentlemen in a more civilized manner than this?"

Frederick Hartley glanced nervously at his friend.

Justin did not raise his eyes from the ground. "No," he replied, barely above a whisper.

"Very well. It's your own funeral," snapped Ashton, hoping, with a touch of malice, to put enough fright into the young man that he might faint dead away. It had happened before.

Hartley's eyes blinked rapidly and he cast a surreptitious look at his friend. Though his shoulders flinched slightly at the harsh words, Justin remained silent.

"As agreed, Hartley, I have engaged the services of a good surgeon," continued Ashton. "Though he naturally wishes to remain removed from these proceedings unless he is needed."

Hartley swallowed and nodded.

The sounds of an approaching rider caused all three heads to jerk around. A large black stallion materialized from the gloom. The rider pulled up next to Ashton's carriage, dismounted, and tossed the reins to the lone coachman standing at the head of the lead pair.

Branford walked purposefully to where the others were standing. His face was impassive, and he merely nodded a curt greeting to Ashton as he came to a halt and began to remove his gloves. Young Hartley swallowed once more as he took in the earl's cool demeanor. Beads of sweat began to form on his brow at the sight of the imposing figure clad in black. He opened his mouth as if to speak, but a quelling look from Justin caused him to reconsider.

Ashton cleared his throat. "As it appears that all attempts to resolve this matter have failed, we shall proceed." He opened the lid of the box to reveal a brace of gleaming, long-barreled pistols. "The pieces have been checked and loaded by me with Mr. Hartley as a witness. Agreed?"

Hartley croaked a yes.

Branford signaled with his eyes to Ashton. The other man frowned slightly, then extended the box toward Hartley and Justin.

"Mr. Chilton, you may choose."

Justin reached out and grasped a weapon with no more than a cursory look. His hand shook slightly.

Ashton offered the remaining one to Branford, who took it up casually, letting his hand fall immediately to his side.

"Hartley and I have marked off the paces. You will move to your spots. When I give the signal, you may fire at will. One shot each."

Both participants took up their positions.

Ashton called "Ready?" and glanced to either side. Both men turned sideways and nodded.

With a muttered oath, he dropped a white handkerchief.

Branford's right arm came up in one swift motion. When it reached shoulder level, he adjusted his aim with a quick, precise movement and pulled the trigger.

Justin's weapon had not yet risen above his waist when he heard the sharp crack. He squeezed his eyes closed very tightly and waited for the inevitable impact. His last thought was of how furious Alex would be at him to let it all end this way. But truly, for honor's sake, he had had no choice.

He almost didn't feel the rush of air as the bullet whizzed past him, so far off the mark it was. His jaw dropped slightly in astonishment and it took an instant for him to absorb the fact that he was indeed unscathed.

Branford's arm dropped to his side and he stood motionless. Even in his black clothes he was clearly visible in the gathering light. Justin's own arm had automatically continued its arc up until it held the gun pointed straight at the earl's chest. All he had to do was take his time and make sure of his aim.

How simple.

So what was the matter with him? he thought as he sighted down the barrel. Why could he not shake the image of Branford's face, naked for that brief moment yesterday morning before his defenses had covered up the look of searing pain? Justin gritted his teeth. Go on, urged an inner voice—the man was a blackguard, a rake, a scoundrel!

Justin jerked his hand slightly to the right and fired.

At the same time, Branford turned straight on to face his adversary, exposing himself more fully to the young man's aim.

"No!" cried Ashton, taking an involuntary step forward.

The bullet tore into Branford with a sickening sound. He staggered backward for a step or two, then collapsed on the ground.

"Sebastian!" Ashton sprinted to his friend and knelt to cradle his head as a dark stain began to spread across the earl's shirt.

Justin threw his pistol to the ground and ran over to Branford's prostrate form. Hartley came up behind him.

Ashton shouted for the surgeon as he pounded his fist onto the ground in frustration.

"Is he . . ." faltered Justin.

Branford's eyes fluttered open. "For God's sake, Henry, get the lads out of here," he whispered weakly. "I depend on you—the doctor shall see to me."

"Sebastian . . ." Ashton began to argue but the earl had already lapsed into unconsciousness. The doctor pushed him aside and hurriedly applied a compress to the wound to staunch the bleeding.

"We must be away from here," he cried, his voice betraying his nervousness. "Help me get him to the carriage."

Ashton called for his coachman and the three of them lifted Branford and carried his limp form to the waiting vehicle. As soon as the door was shut, the coachman tied the reins of the earl's stallion to the back rail, grabbed up the whip, and set the horses off at a gallop.

"In the name of the devil, get moving!" cried Ashton to the others as he retrieved the weapons from the ground. He ran to Hartley's carriage where he none too gently shoved the two dazed young men up the steps toward the dark interior.

"Spring 'em!" he snarled at the terrified driver. Then he climbed in himself and slammed the door.

Every joint of the vehicle creaked and groaned as the wheels bounced over the rutted roads at high speed. For a time, Ashton was content to mutter darkly to himself, casting occasional glowering looks at the two figures hunched on the seat across from him before directing his gaze back at the small side window. Finally, though, he could contain his anger no longer.

"So, are you well pleased with yourself, Chilton?" he asked bitterly. "You have perhaps ended the life of the best man I have had the honor of knowing. A man who has been nothing but a friend to you and your family—for some reason that eludes me, he *liked* you, damn it all. And this is how you repay him! Challenging him to a duel in which his own sense of honor would not allow him to defend himself . . ." he trailed off, smacking his fist into the palm of his other hand. "Damnation!"

Justin's face was deathly pale, his eyes hollow. "I didn't mean . . ." His voice caught in his throat. "The blood, there was so much of it," he whispered. "I . . ." He gave a sudden lurch toward the door. Hartley rapped a signal for the coach to stop. Justin staggered out, fell to his knees, and was violently sick. When he climbed back inside, he slumped against the squabs and lowered his head into his hands.

No one spoke for a time. Finally Hartley, a glazed look still on his features, cast a look bordering on awe at his friend. "Good Lord, Justin," he breathed. "You—you actually bested Lord Branford in a duel."

Justin's head snapped up. "Don't be a gudgeon, Freddy," he said sharply. "We've both seen his lordship shoot. He was off the mark by more than three feet—he missed me on purpose."

"At least you are not stupid as well as foolish," remarked Ashton. He turned to Hartley. "And you, you had better remember your oath of silence about this affair. If I hear even a whisper among the young bucks concerning this morning, you shall answer to me. And I assure you, I will not be as charitable as Branford."

Hartley shrunk back in his seat.

Ashton regarded Justin's haggard face. "Just what was this senseless bloodletting all about?" he demanded. "I have a right to know for what reason my closest friend may give his life."

Justin looked uncomfortable. "I cannot discuss the particulars. But Lord Branford broke his word to me. He promised he would not hurt my sister. He . . . took advantage of her trust—and mine."

Ashton frowned. "I don't believe it. Sebastian would never do such a thing. His code of honor wouldn't allow it."

"But he admitted it," cried Justin. He bit his lip. "He admitted it to her face."

Ashton shook his head doggedly. "I don't care. I know him. It can't be true. He has nothing but . . . the highest regard for your sister."

Justin's hands clenched in his lap. "If he is so honorable, what of the other duels he has fought over a lady's honor?"

"Ah, the infamous duels." Ashton's mouth tightened. "Let me tell you about the first one. The lady in question was my sister-in-law. Her husband proved to be one of those so-called gentlemen who amuse themselves when in their cups by beating their wives. It got even worse when she began increasing. Finally she fled to her sister, my wife, when she feared not only for her own life, but for the life of her unborn child. I was away on the Peninsula campaign. It was Branford who took it upon himself to protect my family. As you well know, the lady had no recourse under the law—she was her husband's chattel, with no more rights than a dog." Ashton's face was rigid with the terrible memory. "Branford caused word to be spread that my sister-in-law was indeed under his protection in every sense of the term. Her husband had no choice but to issue a challenge or be the laughingstock of the *ton*." He took a deep breath. "The world is a better place for the vicious Lord Underhill having taken his leave of it. If you think it dishonorable, would you care to meet a two-year-old with golden curls and a lady who may now venture out of her house without bruises covering her face?"

Justin turned even paler.

"Branford has never allowed me to tell the truth of the tale, for my sister-in-law's sake. I do so now, Mr. Chilton, to show you why I think you are wrong. I trust both of you will honor my insistence that the story never be repeated. And I can assure you, the second duel has an equally compelling explanation."

Justin looked stricken. His head turned to stare out the window, hiding his expression. After a few minutes of silence, Ashton picked up the wooden box beside him and tossed it onto Justin's lap.

"I was told these were for you."

Justin looked totally confused as he fingered the polished brass fastenings. "What do you mean? These are his lordship's—"

"Open it. Didn't you look at them carefully? Those aren't Branford's initials."

Justin picked up one of the beautifully crafted pistols, traces of wet earth still clinging to the bright steel barrel, and regarded the chased silver cap on the butt. The carved initials read *J.T.C.*

"He said he planned to give them to you on your birthday, but that you should have them this morning, as a gentleman should have a decent gun with which to defend his honor." Ashton took grim satisfaction in seeing the young man's jaw twitch uncontrollably. "See to it that you put them to more honorable use in the future," he finished harshly.

The rest of the ride was completed in a miserable silence.

Alex restrained the urge to rip the thick, grained paper into tiny shreds. It was terrible, she thought glumly as she stared at the half-finished painting in front of her. The colors were dull and the curves of the leaves were stiff, as if chiseled out of stone. In a word, it was lifeless. With a sigh, she took the sheet from her easel and slid it away into a portfolio. As she began rinsing out her brushes, she looked over to where her aunt was perusing a rare eighteenth-century translation of Homer.

"I hope Justin is not beginning to associate with the wrong sort of set."

Lady Beckworth laid aside her book and removed her glasses. "Your brother has always shown himself to be an extremely level-headed young man. Has something specific caused you concern?"

Alex hesitated. "Well, I couldn't help but notice that he did not return home at all two nights ago. When he did come in late the next morning, he looked absolutely awful. It appeared as if he hadn't slept at all, his clothes were in disarray and he had, well, he had cast up his accounts as well, by the look of it."

"Young men will occasionally drink more than is good for them and will spend some evenings that they would no doubt like to forget in the morning," counseled her aunt. "Unless it becomes a habit, I shouldn't dwell overmuch on it or mention it. Let him sow a few wild oats."

"No doubt you know best, but I can't help but be concerned." She couldn't add that as well as her concern for his behavior, her fears for his safety had been heightened by what had occurred the night Branford had followed her. If Justin were racketing around town at all hours, doing Lord knew what, the risks were increasing exponentially. She had no doubt that whoever it was would strike again. But when?

"I wish that we could leave London and go home. Things would certainly be less complicated there."

Lady Beckworth gave her a long, searching look. "Justin is becoming a man, my dear. You cannot keep him under your wing forever. Neither of you would wish that."

Alex pressed her lips together. "Yes. I know."

Lady Beckworth let the silence stretch on for a time. Then she spoke again. "Would you care to discuss what it is that is really troubling *you*?"

Alex turned and made a show of carefully arranging her painting materials beside her palette. "What do you mean?"

"I know you think I see no farther than the squiggles on the pages three inches from my nose. But I'm not entirely blind to the real world nor am I completely in my dotage. I simply haven't wanted to pry."

Alex's shoulders sagged. "Oh, Aunt Aurelia, forgive me if I seem ungrateful," she said softly, fighting back tears. "But I don't really wish to speak about anything. It is nothing I cannot handle myself, truly."

"I shan't press you, but sometimes it can feel much better to share your troubles—you needn't carry every burden by yourself, Alex," she said gently.

A knock came on the door.

Justin poked his head in. He had on a freshly pressed shirt and the starched cravat was tied neatly in place but he still looked haggard, his eyes sunken with dark circles under them and his face pale and drawn.

"I shan't be here for supper, and I will not be able to put in an appearance at the Claridge's rout either."

Alex and Lady Beckworth exchanged looks.

"Don't have anyone wait up for me. I shall let myself in by the scullery door. Good evening."

The door closed softly.

Alex bit her lip. She knew who she would have turned to for advice, but that now seemed impossible. After some thought, it occurred to her that she might approach Lord Hammerton. He seemed to have taken an interest in Justin and had spoken with good sense on the dangers that might ensnare a young man new to town. Perhaps she had been hasty in taking an instinctive dislike to the man. After all, he did appear to be a man of taste and refinement. His manners were polished and she was almost sure it was he whom they had overheard voicing concern regarding Branford's behavior.

Yes, talking to Hammerton might be a good idea.

Justin mounted the ornate marble steps of the fashionable town house and, after a brief hesitation, let the knocker fall emphatically on the heavy door.

"Yes, sir?" The butler looked up and down, his expression clearly conveying his opinion of those who called at such an unfashionable hour.

Justin handed his card to the man. "Please inquire whether his lordship will see me despite the hour. It is most pressing."

In a few minutes the butler returned and bade the young man follow him.

Lord Ashton lay down his pen as Justin entered the library and regarded him with a stern countenance. "Well, what is it, Chilton?" he demanded. "I have seen quite enough of your face to suit me for some time."

Justin squared his shoulders. "Yes, my lord, I have no doubt of that. I'm sorry to disturb you at home, but I couldn't bear not knowing—that is, I wanted to know if you would tell me what word you have on—on Lord Branford?"

"A little late for recriminations," admonished Ashton. His eyes narrowed. "Why do you ask? Why should you care, damn it?"

Justin's face took on a look that mirrored his inner turmoil. "I don't understand Lord Branford's actions, but I think I have come to believe that whatever honor demanded, it was not what took place the other morning."

Ashton let out an exasperated sigh as he toyed with the silver inkwell on his desk. "I have been turned away every day. Twice today. He will admit no one. But the doctor says he should recover."

Relief flooded Justin's face. "I am truly glad to hear it." He looked up at Ashton. "I meant to miss, you know," he said softly. "But he moved—"

"Yes, well it seems Sebastian didn't miss where *he* aimed," snapped Ashton sarcastically. "By all rights, you should be lying with your toes cocked up for all your damn headstrong pride."

"I am well aware of that, sir." Justin's gaze fell to the floor. "I cannot blame you for thinking me the veriest of fools, or worse, for all of my actions. I—I don't know quite what to think of myself. You see, everything I have been taught to believe as a gentleman tells me I acted in the right, that honor was served. Yet it feels very hollow—something inside says I was wrong." He raked a hand through his hair and heaved a sigh. "No doubt I sound like a complete sapskull, but even though it seems he betrayed my trust in him, a part of me refuses to believe it is true." The young man's voice caught in his throat. "I wish I could understand it all."

Ashton took a moment to light a cigar. He blew a thick cloud of smoke and watched the rings drift slowly into nothingness. It had taken courage for the young man to face him and admit doubt and error—in fact, few men of his acquaintance, of any age or experience, would have had such honesty. His initial anger began to ebb away, replaced by a grudging respect.

"I see why you remind Sebastian of his cousin. That is a compliment by the way, in case you are tempted to give credence to one of the other filthy rumors. He cared very much for Jeremy."

Justin's gaze remained riveted to the floor but Ashton could detect the slight tremor of his jaw.

At that moment the door opened.

"Oh! Henry, I didn't realize you had company." Cecelia Ashton swept into the room. "Good evening, Mr. Chilton."

She eyed him with a sharp curiosity. It was an odd time to have visitors, especially one who was not on intimate terms with the family.

Justin bowed. "I was just taking my leave, Lady Ashton." Then he turned back to his lordship. "Sir, if I may, I would like to be allowed to call again tomorrow to see if you have any further news."

"Regarding what?" asked Lady Ashton. Very little escaped her notice and the tension in the room was palpable.

Justin colored. "Ah . . ."

Before Ashton could intercede, Lady Ashton fixed him with the expression of a hawk honing in on a sparrow. "Yes, Mr. Chilton? You were saying?"

"Ah . . ." The young man looked around helplessly. Ashton closed his eyes in resignation. "Ah . . . on Lord Branford's condition."

"What is wrong with Sebastian?"

Justin looked at Ashton.

"Henry?"

When her husband didn't answer, she turned back to Justin. He was no match for her piercing stare. After a moment of uncomfortable silence he cleared his throat.

"I'm afraid he's been, well, shot."

"Shot!" exclaimed Lady Ashton. She threw a withering look at her husband.

"Don't blame me, my dear. I did everything in my power to stop it," he mumbled, a defensive look on his harried face.

"And just when were you going to inform me of this?" Lady Ashton placed both hands on her hips. "Damnation, Henry, how is he?"

Lord Ashton winced. "Language, my dear," he reminded, indicating their guest. "He should survive."

"How in heaven's name did this happen?"

Justin colored even more deeply. "I'm afraid I'm to

blame," he answered, unable to look her in the eyes. "I called him out."

Her face flushed with emotion. "This is outside of enough! Kindly explain yourself! Why have you shot one of our dearest friends?"

He took a deep breath. "As I have told your husband, I will not go into particulars, but Lord Branford . . . hurt my sister in the gravest possible manner, after giving me his word he would not toy with her feelings."

Lady Ashton went white. "I don't believe it for an instant, Mr. Chilton."

"Do you think I wish to believe it myself?" exclaimed Justin in a low, pained voice. "But he admitted it when confronted by my sister."

"I think you must go into the particulars, sir, if we are to get to the bottom of this terrible accusation."

Justin shot a confused look at Lord Ashton. "It is not exactly something that can be repeated in front of a lady," he faltered.

"You may rest assured that Lady Ashton is difficult to shock," said Ashton dryly. "When you enter the matrimonial state, you will understand."

Justin still looked hesitant.

Lady Ashton laid a hand on his arm. "Mr. Chilton, you may rest assured that neither my husband nor myself engage in idle gossip. Your sister's privacy is safe with us. And to fathom this disturbing situation we really must know what has happened—we only want to help."

The young man's eyes slid back to the floor. "Lord Branford entered a bet at his club," said Justin, his voice so low as to be barely audible. "The wager was five hundred pounds that—that he could m-m-mount my sister."

Lady Ashton gave a horrified gasp. "No! Sebastian would

never have done such a thing. May I ask how you learned of it?"

"We overheard a private conversation. Two gentlemen who were present were trying to decide just how to warn us."

Lady Ashton gave a dogged shake of her head. "Sebastian would never ruin *any* innocent girl. Never."

"But when Alex asked him if it was true, he said yes."

Lady Ashton's brow furrowed. "There must be an explanation for it."

"What possible explanation could there be for such a thing?" asked Justin, his voice full of anguish.

"I don't know, but I intend to find out." She made for the door.

"Cecelia," exclaimed Lord Ashton. "What do you have in mind?"

"I am going to see Sebastian, of course."

"He won't let you in. I've already tried twice today."

"Hmmph." She gave a toss of her blond curls. "We'll see about that."

"Wait. I shall go with you, if you insist on trying."

"You will do no such thing, Henry."

The door shut with a noise that sounded suspiciously like a slam.

Lord Ashton cast a baleful look at Justin. "I wish you better luck in managing a wife than I seem to have."

For the first time in a while, a ghost of a smile stole to the young man's lips.

"Lord Ashton, if you knew my sister, you would understand that I know exactly what you are up against."

Chapter Eight

Alex glanced distractedly around the room. Mr. Chandler's report on the latest arrival of specimens from the East Indies went unheeded as she searched the crowd for Lord Hammerton. She had almost given up hope of his making an appearance at the ball when finally his sleek, well-groomed head appeared nearby, bent slightly in polite attention to the words of a buxom brunette. Alex shook off a slight feeling of unease. She was no doubt imagining anything amiss beneath the polished manners and immaculate dress. After all, he was a gentleman, and had expressed nothing but solicitous concern for both Justin and herself.

Hammerton solved her dilemma as to how to attract his attention by meeting her gaze almost immediately and making a slight bow of acknowledgment. Disengaging himself from conversation with the lady by his side, he strolled over to where she was standing.

"How pleasant to see you again, Miss Chilton. I have missed you this past week. Have you been well?" He bent over her hand as he spoke, performing the greeting with just the right amount of flourish. A few young men standing nearby eyed his style with a touch of envy.

"I have been . . . occupied," answered Alex.

"Well, I for one am delighted that you have found the time to grace this evening's soiree."

Alex couldn't help but notice that his smile had no real

warmth to it, not like— Stop it, she chided herself. There was little point in dwelling on such thoughts. Besides, it should only serve as a reminder that her judgment concerning people was not as good as she once believed. She forced a smile on her own lips and concentrated on being charming herself—no mean feat.

"How kind of you to notice my absence."

"How could I fail to notice," he replied smoothly. "Now I hope that you will not deprive me of the favor of a dance?"

"I should be delighted."

As she lifted her arm to place her hand on his shoulder, Alex felt a twinge of pain in her injured shoulder and winced slightly.

Hammerton didn't miss the gesture.

"Are you feeling all right, Miss Chilton?" he asked, his voice full of concern.

"Yes, quite. Just a silly accident. It is nothing, really."

He inclined his head a fraction and refrained from inquiring further on the subject.

Really, thought Alex. He is a perfect gentleman.

They exchanged pleasantries throughout the dance, but as the music was ending, Alex turned serious. "My lord, I feel unaccountably warm. Would you be so kind as to accompany me for a short walk in the garden?" In a lower voice she added, "I wish to ask your advice on a most pressing matter, if I may be so bold."

"I should be honored by any confidence you wish to entrust to me," he said earnestly. He took her hand and guided her out through the set of French doors.

Alex felt even more on edge as she walked into the cool evening air on Hammerton's arm. It was worry over Justin she told herself, trying to banish the nagging sense of unease.

"I am very grateful for your concern," she began. "I believe I mentioned to you my fears that the mishaps befalling my brother were no mere accidents?"

Hammerton nodded.

Alex came to a halt where a tall, decorative trellis heavy with tuber roses screened them from any prying ears and eyes. "I now have reason to be *sure* that someone means him harm."

He knitted his brows together. "Truly? That is a serious charge indeed, Miss Chilton. May I ask why?"

"Because last week someone tried to kill me as well."

The words seemed to shock him. He took a half step backward, as if recoiling from a physical blow. "Perhaps—I mean no offense—perhaps you are magnifying an incident in light of your understandable concern for your—"

"A gunshot leaves little to the imagination," interrupted Alex, a little more sharply than she wished.

"No, it does not." He rubbed his chin, as if in deep thought. Alex was relieved of some of her anxiety by the fact that he seemed to be taking her seriously at last.

"Have you discussed your concerns with anyone else? I have noticed that Lord Branford seems to be a friend . . ." He let the sentence die on a note of question.

Alex carefully schooled her features to remain impassive, "Lord Branford is merely an acquaintance who has a passing interest in botany. He is not one I would discuss personal matters with, while you, sir, have kindly expressed an interest in Justin. If I have overstepped—"

"Not at all." In the shadowed recesses of the overhanging foliage Alex missed the slight smile of satisfaction that passed fleetingly over Hammerton's face. In an instant it was gone, replaced by an expression more befitting the gravity of the situation. "You were quite right to speak to me, Miss Chilton. Your brother is an amiable young man and I am happy to be of service to you and your family in trying to put an end to this nasty business." He paused and regarded her with a strange intensity. "Tell me, have you any idea why anyone would want to harm either of you?"

"No!" All of her frustration and confusion combined to make the word sound suspiciously like a wail, though it was barely louder than a whisper.

Hammerton mistook its origins and patted her arm soothingly. She restrained the urge to flick his fingers away. He meant it kindly, she knew, yet his touch was oddly repellent. For some reason she did not make mention of her father's letter. It really was of no import anyway.

"I am not without contacts with which to pursue an investigation of this matter," he continued in a silky tone. "I shall begin making discreet inquiries immediately and will keep you informed as to what I discover."

Alex breathed a sigh of relief. It appeared her trepidation concerning the man was as misplaced as her earlier trust.

"Thank you, sir. I am very much in your debt."

Hammerton touched her arm once more. "You have come to the right person, I assure you, Miss Chilton." The same chilling smile crept back to his lips. "And now perhaps it would be wise for us to return to the ballroom before any idle tongues are set to wagging."

A true gentleman, Alex had to admit as she let herself be led back into the glittering lights and festive mood.

Cecelia Ashton marched up the front steps of the magnificent town house and brought the heavy knocker down with a bang.

Once. Twice, Three times. Her foot tapped impatiently on the ornate landing as she waited for Branford's footman to open the massive oak door.

When he did finally crack it enough to observe the unexpected visitor, his face barely masked his surprise at seeing a lone female—and a diminutive one at that—seeking admittance at such an hour.

"Kindly open the door. I am in no mood to tarry here on the doorstep all evening," snapped Lady Ashton.

For a moment, the man looked utterly nonplussed at being spoken to in such a manner. Then, recovering his equilibrium, he replied to the demand in a stentorian voice. "I am sorry, madam, but Lord Branford is not at home."

"Fustian!" With the point of her neatly furled parasol, she pushed the door wide open. The footman moved his rather large form to block the entrance.

"Madam!" he intoned again, though his inflection indicated his doubt as to whether she was deserving of such polite address. "I repeat, Lord Branford is *not* receiving visitors."

The parasol came down hard on his shins. With an undignified yelp, he recoiled sideways, allowing Lady Ashton to sweep by.

"Is he in the library?" Her head was already poking into the darkened room. "No. I take it, then, he is in his bedchamber?"

The man made a strangled sound.

"You needn't fear any repercussions," she said airily as she ascended the stairs. "I shall inform Lord Branford you had no choice in the matter."

At the top of the landing she hesitated. On the right, a door was ajar and the faint light of a single candle was barely discernible. She entered very quietly.

Branford lay under a light coverlet, his eyes closed. His white linen shirt, open at the throat, heightened the pallor of his skin, evident even under the rough stubble of his unshaven chin and tangle of uncombed locks. Without opening his eyes, he gave a faint smile. "Poor Hawkins was no match for you, I see, Cecelia."

She dropped her parasol and came to the edge of the bed. "Oh, Sebastian." Her hand smoothed a tangle of hair from his brow and she brushed a quick kiss on his heated cheek.

He shifted slightly, wincing involuntarily at the pain that shot through his side.

"Are you badly hurt?" Lady Ashton asked as she moved the coverlet down to expose his chest. Through the fine weave of his garment she could see the heavy bandage wrapped under his breast.

"No vital organs damaged. Just a nick to the ribs. The doctor says I am lucky." He gave a harsh laugh. "I wish I could feel the same."

Lady Ashton moved a chair so she might sit by his side. "My dear friend," she said softly, taking up his limp hand and holding it to her cheek. "You were there for me in my time of need. My sister and her child would not be alive if not for you—"

He cut her off. "I only did what Henry would have done."

"But Henry wasn't there! You defended her from that blackguard. Now, when you are in need, let me help you."

"I am beyond help," he said bleakly.

Lady Ashton squared her shoulders. "Nonsense," she said forcefully. "Though how a man of your intelligence managed to get himself in such a coil is beyond me. Kindly explain this ridiculous bet."

Branford's eyes shot wide open. "How the devil—"

"Justin Chilton is no match for me either. He is, by the way, feeling quite wretched over this."

"I hope you weren't too hard on him. He did what any loyal brother must have done under the circumstances."

"I didn't have to be—he is doing a good enough job on his own. Henry wouldn't admit it, but I think even he was moved by the boy's courage in coming to our house to find out how you were."

In spite of himself, Branford smiled briefly. "He's a good lad."

"Yes, I think he is, but don't try to evade my question. I'm not leaving here until I get a satisfactory answer."

"That I can well believe," murmured Branford. He gave a deep sigh, only to have it cut short by another spasm of pain wracking his chest.

Lady Ashton's hand tightened on his.

"Very well," he said in a tone of resignation. "I was deep in my cups some weeks back—knowing Henry, I'm sure he voiced his concern over what he termed my destructive behavior. I had stopped at my club at a very late hour after—another sort of indulgence I needn't go into. A group of gentlemen were having a discussion. Alex's name came up as someone no better than she should be. I don't even recall exactly how it happened but I let myself be drawn into a bet, of which you have heard the unsavory particulars. As soon as I met Alex, I realized she was . . . she was an innocent, not the experienced, worldly lady I had been tricked into pursuing."

"Sebastian! How could you be such a ninnyhammer!" Lady Ashton's tone of exasperation reverberated throughout the room.

"I admit it was not the most gentlemanly thing, no matter what the reputation of the lady involved. I think you know I usually would not let—"

"That's not what I meant. Why the devil didn't you tell Alex this?"

"I—I—" A look of acute embarrassment flooded his normally stoic face. He let his eyes fall closed again. "I don't quite know." He looked lost. "I suppose I was hurt that she didn't believe enough in me to know I would never hurt her."

"Believe you would never hurt her," repeated Lady Ashton incredulously. "My God, how unfair of you! She believed enough in you to become your friend. Then a vicious rumor comes to her attention. What is she to think, indeed? Instead of falling into a fit of vapors, she does what any intelligent young lady should do—she asks you the truth! And you, you had too much foolish pride to trust she would understand. Why, it is *you* who did not believe in *her* enough!"

She made a sound of exasperation. "Ohhh, I could shoot you myself," she muttered, causing Branford's lips to quirk for a moment into a harried smile before falling back into an expression of hopelessness.

"Well, at least you did not actually . . ."

His chin sunk to his chest.

"Sebastian, you didn't!"

A tinge of color washed the pallor from his face.

"Oh dear."

"Cecelia," he stammered. "It is not what you might imagine. It . . . well, it is rather impossible to explain what led to—damnation! Fetch my coat over there."

Lady Ashton raised her eyebrows in question but went to retrieve the garment.

"Look in the pocket."

She took out a folded sheet of paper.

"Read it."

She opened it and quickly scanned its contents. "It's a special license."

"I meant to ask her that morning."

Lady Ashton was silent for a moment. "Because honor demanded it?"

"No," he said in barely a whisper. "Because I love her, and the prospect of life without her seems intolerable."

Lady Ashton's expression softened. "I am happy to see your intelligence has not deserted you entirely, Sebastian. The two of you will suit. I like her very much—she has enough sense and spirit to manage you quite well!" She smiled as she finished her words and squeezed his hand. "I wish you happy. And I truly believe you will be."

Branford finally opened his eyes. Their rich sapphire color was clouded with despair. "But I have made an impossible mull of it. No doubt she must hate me, and with ample reason. I fear I have lost her."

"No doubt she is very angry with you. And very hurt." She patted his arm. "That has nothing to do with love. I have seen her watch you in a crowded room, Sebastian. Things are not as hopeless as you think."

He looked at her with disbelief.

"Men!" she muttered under her breath. "I see I shall have to have a little chat with Miss Chilton tomorrow so we may begin to set things right," she continued in a firmer tone.

"No!" cried Branford, rising up on one elbow, despite the pain in his side. "I mean, I cannot allow you to make explanations for my behavior—it would be more than cowardly. She must hear the truth from my own lips."

"Of course," agreed Lady Ashton. "I have no intention of explaining the particulars—she would neither want nor welcome it from me. I merely mean to have a little tête-à-tête with her concerning how brainless men are at times." She smiled sweetly. "It is fortunate you have other charms to make up for it."

In spite of himself, Branford could not suppress a low chuckle. "You are impossible, Cecelia."

"So Henry tells me." She rose and planted another light kiss on his forehead. "Try to rest tonight and gather your strength. Somehow, I have the distinct feeling you are going to need it."

Hammerton was feeling extraordinarily lucky. Sure enough, the dice came up favorably again. Yes, he was on a roll.

Around him, other men in various stages of inebriation muttered curses at his good fortune and drifted away to other tables. He raked his winnings across the green baize and stuffed them into his pocket as his eyes sought to penetrate the smoky haze enveloping the gaming hell.

He spotted Standish in a corner, a doxy on his lap, her skirts already pushed up around her ample thighs. His hands were roaming over her chest where the thin material of her gown made only the barest pretense of covering her breasts. As Hammerton approached, he could see his cousin's hips rocking up and down, his head lolling back and his breath coming faster and faster.

"I must speak with you immediately," he said, coming up behind Standish's chair.

Standish froze. "Now?" he cried incredulously.

A malicious smile crossed Hammerton's face as he observed the effect of his presence. The girl shifted slightly, then slipped from Standish's lap.

"P'rhaps later," she said with a saucy grin.

"Couldn't this have waited a few more minutes?" whined his cousin as he took a silk handkerchief from his pocket and wiped the perspiration from his brow.

"Button yourself and come with me. You will be pleased enough to kiss my boots rather than that tart's nipple when you hear what I have to tell you."

With one hand firmly on the other man's elbow, Hammerton guided him toward the door, brushing aside an older gentleman who was groping a girl scarcely older than thirteen. Of all the establishments catering to the appetites of men with money, this was one of the more disreputable, so there was little chance of being recognized by anyone from proper Society. Nonetheless, Hammerton hurried Standish through the cool night air and bade him climb in the waiting carriage.

"I'm not finished for the night. Couldn't we have talked in there?"

Hammerton rapped on the trap and the carriage moved off.

"I need you with your wits about you tomorrow." He steepled his fingers and a self-satisfied look spread over his features as he regarded his companion. "A most fortuitous thing has happened." He recounted what had taken place earlier in the evening. "Isn't it rich—I am now her protector. She trusts me implicitly."

Standish's jaw dropped in astonishment. Hammerton gave a harsh laugh.

"You wanted the matter resolved quickly? I assure you, by tomorrow night, she and her damnable brother will be a problem for us no longer. The plan couldn't be simpler . . ."

He leaned forward and the two of them conversed in low tones for the rest of the ride back to Hammerton's town house.

Alex moved desultorily around the library. Her eyes were dull with lack of sleep, and she knew that any attempt at painting would only culminate in a result even more depressing than inactivity. Instead, she busied herself with straightening up the library. The table was strewn with papers and stacks of books which she began to arrange into neat piles. When she came to her father's letter she paused, studying its meaningless letters and strange symbols with a rising sense of frustration. She couldn't shake the feeling that somehow their current troubles were linked in some way with their father's odd penchant for secrecy. With a silent oath, she threw it onto the nearest pile and turned to reorganizing her portfolio.

As she arranged the plants according to genus and species, her hands stopped at the hibiscus. She made herself look at it. It was one of her strongest works, the form and color infused with a vitality that nearly made the petals and leaves sprout up off the paper. A tear or two appeared, unbidden, and she wiped them away with the sleeve of her gown. Perhaps he would still like to have it, even though he had not fulfilled his end of the bargain. That is, of course, assuming his admiration was not feigned, not merely part of the game. She knew she would never be able to look at it without hearing his rich baritone voicing its praises or seeing in her mind's eye the warmth of his sapphire eyes as he glanced from her easel to her face.

Damnation, it was his eyes that haunted her. The way they had looked at her in the candlelight, the depth of emotion they had revealed in the moment before his own release, as if allowing her to see into the vulnerable, unsure self that he kept submerged so deep within. Everything between them—from the heated discussions to the laughter to the gentle touch of his fingers as he dressed her wound—seemed real. And yet, she had heard the single, stark word spoken that consigned all of it to being no more than illusion. Her intellect accepted that she had been manipulated by one whose skills at dissemblement far surpassed her ability to discern it. But her heart still fought against believing it.

"Alex?" Lady Beckworth's voice floated through the door.

Alex smoothed her gown, brushed her sleeve once more over her eyes, and forced a bright look.

"Yes, I'm here."

Lady Beckworth poked her head in. "Oh. You are at work early."

Her gaze lingered on Alex's wan face with some concern before she continued speaking. "A note arrived for you just now." The door opened the rest of the way to admit her frail form and she handed the folded paper to her niece.

Alex regarded the unfamiliar handwriting with a slight frown before she broke the seal.

Dear Miss Chilton,
I have discovered some extraordinary news concerning the matter we discussed last night. Until I have a chance to explain, I think it best to maintain absolute secrecy and discretion. If you will take a walk at 10 this morning, a hackney cab will pick you up at the entrance to Green Park and bring you to me.
Yours, etc.
Hammerton

Carefully schooling her features to reveal no emotion, she tucked the letter into her bodice. In answer to her aunt's inquiring look, she said, "Mr. Simpson has managed to procure a few of the prized specimens that arrived from the East Indies last week. Perhaps I shall go to see them later."

Lady Beckworth looked as if to say something but Alex turned and began busying herself with cleaning her palette and brushes. Lips pressed together, her aunt took herself off to confer with Cook over the supper menu.

An hour later, Alex left the house alone.

Lady Ashton's carriage rolled to a stop before the modest town house. Moving with even greater alacrity than normal, she mounted the steps and knocked impatiently on the door. An elderly servant finally answered the summons.

"Kindly inform Miss Chilton that Lady Ashton wishes to see her on a most urgent matter."

The servant blinked. "Miss Alex is not at home."

Lady Ashton pursed her lips. She had called at the earliest possible hour that manners allowed. Where could the girl have gone off to?

"Do you know when she will return?"

The man shook his head.

"Please tell her I shall return this afternoon." She put her card on the silver tray the man was holding patiently in front of him. "And do not forget to add that it is most important I see her." Lady Ashton did not like her plans, once put into action, to be thwarted, but she had no choice. It seemed she would have to wait until later.

Branford gingerly swung his legs to the floor and stood up slowly. Though feeling a trifle unsteady, the dizziness and nausea had passed—as had his despair. Satisfied, he rang for his valet. Freshly shaved and dressed, he felt even more like a new man. At least there was a glimmer of hope, he thought with a rueful smile as he recalled Lady Ashton's visit. When she put her mind to it, anything—even untangling the coil he had gotten himself into—was possible. And what's more, she had made him realize what a coward he had been. It wasn't like him to give up and retreat without a fight. Cecelia was right—Alex deserved better from him. The resolve gave spring to his step. Throwing a silk dressing gown over his shirt, he made his way downstairs.

He went right to his study, asking for coffee and toast to be brought there. Something about the letter Alex had given him had been hovering at the edges of his consciousness throughout his feverish state. While he waited for news from Lady Ashton, he determined to have another look at it. He removed the copy Alex had made from his desk drawer, along with the sheaf of notes he had made during his trip to East Anglia. Spreading the pieces of paper out over the entire desktop reminded him of the jigsaw puzzles he had played with as a child. The analogy seemed apt. All the pieces were here, he was sure.

He just had to figure out how they went together.

Alex hesitated before the nondescript coach.

"Be ye Miss Chilton?" growled the driver.

She nodded and he jerked his head to indicate she should climb inside. With a quick look around to satisfy herself that no one was taking any notice, she quickly obeyed. A flick of the whip set the horses in motion. Inside the musty interior Alex could barely make out the passing sights through the small, grimy window. She could tell they were heading east, but she soon lost all sense of bearing as the hackney threaded its way through a maze of increasingly seedy streets until it finally came to a halt by a deserted alleyway. Two razor-thin dogs fighting over an old leather boot were the only signs of life save for another carriage. It was painted entirely black, with no markings to distinguish it. Even the coachman blended in seamlessly with it, dressed head to toe in the same somber color, a voluminous cloak drawn around him and a slouched hat pulled low over his eyes. Four powerful horses stomped impatiently at the rutted mud.

"Yer ta git out here," said Alex's driver.

She wrenched the door open and climbed down, well glad to be out of the dank space. The door of the other carriage swung open. The interior was as inky as the one she had just left, causing her to stop momentarily amid the broken crates and decaying garbage. Behind her the chink of coins jingled as her driver caught a leather purse tossed to him by the other coachman. The hackney immediately rattled off, leaving her little choice but to walk toward the waiting carriage.

A gloved hand reached out of the shadowed recesses to assist her up.

"Your pardon, Miss Chilton, for such an unpleasant start," came a disembodied voice.

"Lord Hammerton." Alex's tone betrayed a touch of relief as well as annoyance. "Pray, sir, was this really necessary? Surely you could have met me in a less out-of-the-way place without attracting undue attention."

"You will soon see the necessity of it, I assure you," he answered smoothly.

Alex settled herself into the seat facing him and wasted no time in getting down to business. Her nerves, already frayed dangerously thin, were in no state for beating around the bush.

"What have you learned?" she demanded.

Hammerton smiled inwardly. "Please be patient, Miss Chilton. I had rather arrive at our destination before beginning an explanation."

"Have you learned the identity of whoever is trying to harm my brother?"

"Indeed I have. And you shall soon know it too. Trust me, Miss Chilton."

Alex leaned back and bit her lip to cut off any of the sharp retorts that came to mind. She had, after all, put herself in his hands and supposed she must curb her own inclinations to immediate action. He must know what he was about, especially if he had succeeded in discovering who was behind all their troubles in just one night. Still, she was acutely uncomfortable. Perhaps it was the gloomy atmosphere inside the cab. The curtains had been drawn, emitting so little light that she could barely see her own hands clenched tightly in her lap. Hammerton's face was merely a black silhouette, devoid of all expression. She gave a tiny shudder. It reminded her of being in a tomb.

The carriage came to an abrupt halt. Hammerton stuck his

head out the door, made a quick signal, then waved for the driver to move on.

"What—" began Alex.

"I promise you, it will all soon be clear."

Hammerton made no further effort at conversation. His shoulders set as if he were napping, or at least in deep thought, and Alex could think of nothing she wanted to say anyway, except to demand to know what was going on. Matching his own demeanor, she hunched into the squabs and closed her eyes. However she could also not refrain from gritting her teeth.

After what seemed like an interminably long time, Alex could stand it no longer. She sat up and yanked one of the curtains open. To her surprise, they were now well out of the city.

"Lord Hammerton, where are we going?"

"As I said, you shall soon see."

The answer and the tone in which it was delivered were entirely unsatisfactory.

"I am in no mood to continue this," she snapped. "I demand to know where we are going and why."

The light was now strong enough for her to see the smile that crossed his face. It sent a chill through her very bones.

"Stop the carriage this instant!"

His smile only broadened.

"Stop!" she cried, striving to be heard over the clatter of the wheels.

"You needn't bother yelling," he drawled. "The driver is my cousin and I assure you no amount of noise from you will cause him the least anxiety." As he spoke he negligently removed a pistol from the pocket of his greatcoat. "Now kindly sit back. I would prefer not to shoot you quite yet, but if you force me, I promise you my shot will not just graze you this time."

Comprehension dawned on her. "You!" she whispered.

"Brilliant, my dear Miss Chilton," he sneered as he pantomimed clapping his hands together. The pistol waved lazily back and forth in the air, always pointed at her chest.

Alex felt a hollowness in the pit of her stomach. Good Lord, had she really been so stupid? And what of Justin? she thought with rising panic.

As if reading her thoughts, Hammerton continued. "You asked where I am taking you. I have a small hunting box that only very few people know about. When we stopped earlier, it was to signal that everything was going according to plan. A note has by now been delivered to your dear brother, who will nobly follow it to the letter in hopes of seeing you alive."

"He won't—he's not that foolish."

Hammerton gave a nasty laugh. "Of course he'll come. And he'll come alone."

Alex's eyes squeezed shut. To her dismay, she felt a burning sensation against her lids. Blinking rapidly, she brushed it away. She wasn't ready to give up just yet. Her chin came up.

"Why?"

His mouth quirked in anticipation. Clearly he had been itching to reveal just how clever he was.

"Of course. You wish to know what all of this is about." He stopped to savor the sweet taste of his triumph. "Well, there is little enough harm now in telling you the whole story."

Alex was growing heartily sick of the look of smug satisfaction plastered on his slick features, but she kept her tongue in check. She needed to know what he was going to tell her if she had any hope of devising a way out of this coil—

"First of all, I am not the Earl of Hammerton."

Alex's eyes registered her surprise. He greeted her reaction with another bark of laughter, causing her to wish she could plant her fist squarely on those thin, bloodless lips.

"That is," he amended, "I am not the true Earl of Hammerton. That title rightfully belongs to your brother, now that your father is dead."

Alex couldn't repress a gasp.

"Yes," he remarked. "We have a very odd and exasperating family, do we not, Miss Chilton. We are cousins, you know. How charming."

When she did not let herself be goaded into a reply he merely shrugged and went on.

"I was raised by my great-uncle, who took me in as a child after my parents had died during an outbreak of influenza. Despite two marriages, he never managed to produce an heir, so it was natural that as time went on, everyone considered that I was to be the next Earl of Hammerton. My earliest recollections were those of a rather, shall we say, meager childhood. My side of the family had no money and no prospects. So I very quickly became used to my . . . new position in life." He paused to flick a speck of lint from the lapel of his immaculately tailored jacket. "*Very* used to it." He regarded Alex with a humorless smile. "It is quite pleasant to have enough money to indulge in one's fancies—and enough influence to make sure any indiscretion is glossed over." His expression grew harder. "To think the old rotter would imagine I'd willingly give it up. For he did, you know."

He stopped and Alex watched in disgust as his eyes narrowed to mere slits, like those of a snake, as he contemplated the past.

"He was taken quite ill, and at his advanced years it was feared he might not recover. I suppose the prospect of meeting his Maker finally brought on an attack of conscience.

God knows the damn fellow showed no generosity of spirit during his lifetime—what he couldn't manipulate or control he crushed. Except for me, of course. I was too smart for him, even as a child. Oh, I played his game. It cost very little to pretend obedience when measured against the rewards."

Hammerton sat back and gave a mocking smile. "Your father, on the other hand, was apparently as bull-headed as the old earl. Stubborn, proud, and unwilling to bend an inch—how extraordinarily stupid."

"What do you mean?" she asked, though he needed no prodding to continue his terrible account.

"Your father's side of the family, the next in the line of succession, was as badly dipped as mine. As I have said, Uncle gave nothing without expecting an even greater payment in return. Your father was much older than I was when the earl sought him out. From what I gather, he would not knuckle under to the old tyrant's demands that he live under his thumb. Both were volatile by nature. Ugly words were exchanged and your father stormed from the house, consigning both title and fortune to the devil. He vowed never to have contact with the earl again and never to touch a farthing of his."

Alex drew her breath in. How very like her father, she thought with a mixture of exasperation and grudging respect. But most of all, she felt sorrow for him, at the bitter battle that must have raged inside him between his own cursed pride and his guilt at depriving his son of his rightful place in the world.

"But I digress," continued Hammerton. "My uncle called me to his sickbed to inform me that he meant to make amends for his past sins by reconciling with his true heir—your father. I believe he had come to know of your brother's existence and suddenly felt compelled to do his duty and see that the title passed on to the rightful branch of the family. That, and perhaps rumors had reached him regarding certain aspects of my behavior in town."

Again the lips curled upward, sending a chill down Alex's spine. "He assured me that he would see to it that I was well taken care of, that there was enough blunt for both your father and me. I would receive a settlement that would allow me to continue living in the style to which I had became accustomed. Hah! He had no idea what sort of things I had become accustomed to! And reverting to a mere 'mister' was most definitely not one of them."

A silence stretched out for what felt like ages to Alex as Hammerton fell into a reverie, his features twisted with malevolent satisfaction as he seemed to savor the recollection of his triumph over anyone who sought to thwart his will. She almost believed he had forgotten her presence when he looked up, his eyes glittering with that expression she had come to hate.

"So just like that," he said, "I was told that I was no longer to think of becoming the fifth Earl, that I must step aside for your father. Give up *my* title, *my* estates, *my* fortune to someone who hadn't paid for them like I had, to a recluse who spent his time picking weeds? Not bloody likely!"

His voice had risen to an agitated pitch. "It was simple, really. A pillow placed over his face for a matter of a few minutes. The old bird scarcely had the strength to flap his arms. It was with great sorrow that I announced to the servants that dear Uncle had expired in my arms."

Alex shot him a look of pure disgust, but he seemed not to notice.

"Unfortunately, he had already written to your father, who had agreed to meet with him after all these years. Naturally, I had to take care of that as well. Knowing your father had a son who was drawing close to adulthood, I feared that was reason enough for him to change his mind."

Alex sucked in her breath, somehow knowing what was coming. Even so, the sheer effrontery of his manner left her reeling.

"I believe your father had become a bit suspicious over dear Uncle's untimely death. He left his inn late that night to return home, but he was not, shall we say, a member of the Four-In-Hand Club, and his cattle weren't fit for a farmer's dray. It was remarkably easy to nudge his carriage off the road just as it curved out over the cliffs—my matched bays hardly broke stride." He gave a pained sigh. "I was reasonably sure you and your dottering aunt knew nothing. But when I learned that your brother was not content to remain a country oaf but had entered Oxford, and had plans to come to town for this Season, I knew he would have to be dealt with as well. I couldn't risk him ever stumbling across the truth."

Given the strength, Alex would gladly have throttled the life out of him.

The smug look had returned to his face. "I have never lost a match of wits, Miss Chilton. It is a pity you tried to put your feeble female mind up against mine. Admit it, I am a superior intellect. I have bent all of you to my own design, including that cur, Branford."

"I find you akin to *Spirogyra*."

Hammerton looked faintly perplexed, not quite sure of the meaning. Alex let him ponder it for a moment before she said slowly, "It is Latin. For pond algae. Though I regret to insult the plant phylum with comparison to you—perhaps a reptile would be more apt."

His hand flashed out, catching her across the cheek with a blow hard enough to daze her.

"Shut up, you bitch," he spat. "You will soon regret your actions."

She already had, she thought miserably. If only she had—but what was the use in flaying herself over things that could not be undone? She set her teeth and put her mind to coming up with some way out of the nightmare.

She could only pray Justin would display more sense than she had.

Chapter Nine

The blow connected squarely on his chin, sending him sprawling onto his backside. "Justin!" Hartley extended a hand and helped his friend to his feet. "Sorry, but you must truly be woolgathering to let me plant such a facer."

One of the attendants of the famed boxing establishment glowered at them. "That's enough fer you lads. If Gentleman Joe were to witness that 'orrible display of skill I reckon you'd be thrown out on yer ear."

Red-faced at the set-down, Justin and Hartley slunk off to dress, enduring a gamut of friendly jibes from others waiting to go a few rounds.

"Forgive me, Freddy," said Justin as he toweled off and reached for his shirt. "I fear I have not been the best of company for the past few days."

Hartley shrugged. "No need to apologize." He looked around quickly then spoke in a much lower voice. "Have you heard any further word? I take it we will not be having to flee the country?"

Justin shook his head. He realized with a pang of guilt that he had caused his friend no little anxiety. Dueling was, after all, illegal and if Branford had been killed they would have been in very serious trouble—poor Freddy must have endured some sleepless nights as well.

"No, thank God," he answered in a near whisper. "It appears he will recover."

Hartley knotted his cravat with a sigh of relief. "Well, in that case, there is no need to be so blue-deviled, man. Come, we'll stop by the club, then there is a cockfight I've gotten word about that promises to be most entertaining. And of course we'll put in an appearance at the Creighton's soiree."

Justin nodded glumly and finished dressing. Perhaps Freddy was right and it was best to keep occupied. However he still couldn't seem to banish his low spirits.

As the two of them headed for the street, an attendant approached.

"Excuse me, Mr. Chilton. A man left this for you. Said I was to give it to you when you was leaving." He extended a sealed note.

Justin broke the wafer and quickly ran his eyes over the contents.

"Freddy, you must excuse me," he said as he fumbled in his pocket and pressed a coin in the man's outstretched hand.

"Is something—" began Hartley, but Justin had already disappeared out the door.

Once on the street, Justin began walking blindly, at a pace that drew reproving looks from the number of gentlemen he shouldered past. Heedless of anything save for the words etched on the paper, his mind was racing as fast as his limbs.

The note read:

If you wish to see your sister alive again, be at the crossroads two miles east of the village of Weston at 6 tonight. Come alone, or else.

She had been right after all. Swearing silently, he wished he had taken Alex's warnings more seriously. It had been convenient to dismiss them as the exaggerated worries of an overprotective older sister even though, at heart, he had known it was highly improbable that the accidents were mere coincidences. But it had seemed absurd that someone would try to harm him—what possible threat was he to anyone?

That was at the heart of the matter. Wrack his brain though he might, he could find no plausible explanation. And now, with Alex entangled in the web of intrigue, he still had no idea of how to begin unraveling the mystery. But the one thing he did know was that he would be damned if he would ride meekly to his appointed doom. Besides, Alex would be furious with him if he were to be so corkbrained as to fall into such an obvious trap without trying to figure out a way to best this shadowy nemesis.

He made himself think.

It suddenly occurred that the first step should be to make sure it wasn't a complete trick, that he didn't run off willy-nilly without ascertaining that Alex was in fact gone. He flagged a passing hansom and hurried back to Half Moon Street.

Forcing some semblance of composure, he took a deep breath and entered the library. "Aunt Aurelia, have you seen Alex?"

His aunt looked up from her book. "No. Givens said she left here earlier this morning and she has not returned." There was a note of concern in her voice. "She received a note first thing. She said it was from Mr. Simpson regarding an invitation to view some newly arrived plants—but she was acting most strangely." She rose from her chair, her frail hands clasped tightly together. "Something has been quite wrong lately. Justin, do you know what it is that has Alex so upset?"

He took another deep breath. "I have an inkling."

Lady Beckworth was near tears. "Is everything going to be all right?"

Justin gave her a swift hug. "You may count on it," he promised, though he wished he felt as sanguine as his words. "I have to go now, but don't worry. I'll find her. No doubt we will both be home for supper."

As she watched him disappear down the hallway she bit her lip in worry. She could only pray that he would make the right decisions.

Once out on the street, Justin began walking at a furious pace again. Think, he cajoled himself. Think!

Alex was clever. What would she do?

He considered his options. He had no idea how to begin uncovering the identity of his enemy or where to start looking for where he had Alex hidden. That did not make for a very auspicious beginning, he thought to himself with a grim set of his jaw. On top of that, he had no illusions as to the intent of the note's author—or his willingness to carry out his threat. He had shown that all too clearly in the past. No, whoever it was meant to kill both Alex and himself. The meeting tonight was nothing more than a lure to reel him in as well. But with the lure in the form of his sister, he had no choice but to rise to the bait.

Or did he?

He stopped dead in his tracks, drawing an acid comment from the young dandy who collided into his back. Stepping aside with mumbled apologies, Justin began to walk again, slowly and deliberately. It was a crazy idea—he was mad to even consider it. But he could think of nothing else.

Time was precious, and he had to do something.

Justin rushed up the town house steps and rapped hurriedly on the door. It opened just wide enough for a pair of wary eyes to ascertain who was seeking admittance. Once satisfied that it was not a certain, diminutive lady, the footman abandoned his rather undignified position of using the massive piece of oak as shield and drew himself up to his full, imperious height.

"His lordship is not—"

Justin elbowed him aside. "I must see him!"

The footman seemed to measure who might come out on top in a battle of fisticuffs—at least here was an opponent against whom he had a fighting chance. He took a step toward the young man, who had stopped in the entrance hall, unsure of where to go from there.

"A life may depend on it," entreated Justin.

The other man hesitated. What had been a well-run, disciplined household had been at sixes and sevens for the last few days, and the earl, normally a stickler for obedience, had tolerated some peculiar intrusions. Seeing as he hadn't lost his position over the past evening, he sighed and motioned Justin to follow him down a long hallway, then left him in front of the closed door of the study with a silent indication that his lordship was within. Regardless of the liberties allowed recently, he was not about to open the earl's inner sanctorum himself—the young man was on his own from there.

Suddenly Justin's mouth went dry. He felt all too keenly the awkwardness of his situation. It was one thing to have made a spur-of-the-moment decision on the street, quite another to now be faced with seeing it through.

What would he say?

By all rights, he should expect to be thrown out on his ear. But he bucked up his courage by reminding himself that was the worst that could happen to him—then he thought about Alex and what could happen to her.

Swallowing the lump in his throat, he opened the door and crossed the threshold.

Branford looked up from his papers.

"Chilton." He appeared surprised, but not unpleasantly so. "Pray, come in."

"Excuse my intrusion, sir, especially since—that is, I . . ." He gave up searching for polite words. "Alex has been kidnapped," he blurted out. "I don't know what to do. I—I thought perhaps you might help me."

Branford shot to his feet, ignoring the pain in his side. "Bloody hell!" he said through gritted teeth. "When?"

"It must have been sometime this morning." He took the folded note out of his pocket and thrust it at the earl. "I received this at Jackson's as I was leaving not half an hour ago."

Branford read it, then crumpled it in his fist.

"I've checked at home, to be sure," added Justin. "She left the house alone and has not returned."

"Marlowe," he roared. "Bring me my jacket and greatcoat—and my pistols. Have Sykes harness the grays and bring the carriage around immediately!"

Justin hung his head. "I'm afraid, sir, that I have no idea where to begin looking for her, or who is behind all of this—"

"Oh, but I bloody do," growled the earl as he took the young man by the shoulder and propelled him toward the door.

Once in the carriage, Branford immediately set to checking the priming of his weapons. The grim set of his jaw discouraged Justin from saying a word until the earl rapped on the trap and called out a destination.

"White's?" repeated Justin faintly.

Branford appeared not to hear him but kept his attention focused on ensuring the pistols were in perfect working order. Only when the horses came to a halt in the middle of St. James's Street did he look up.

"Wait for me here," he ordered curtly as he made to get out.

"But my lord," cried Justin involuntarily. "Surely you can't mean to enter White's at this hour with a brace of pistols—"

The earl's expression caused him to swallow the rest of his words.

It was no longer than ten minutes before Branford returned, a look of grim satisfaction on his pale face. He spoke briefly with Sykes before climbing back into the carriage. A spasm of pain crossed his features as he eased himself in against the squabs. It didn't escape Justin's notice. Their eyes met and remained locked for a moment. Strangely, it was Branford who turned away to stare out the window.

The janglings of the harness mixed with the cries of the costermongers and bustle of the streets as Sykes set the horses to as fast a pace as could be managed. Even with one hand missing, he handled the ribbons with skill. Soon the team was racing toward the outskirts of the city.

Justin finally summoned the nerve to break the silence. "Sir, I wish to speak to you regarding our . . . last meeting."

Branford turned to look at him, an inscrutable expression on his drawn face.

"I truly regret having caused you injury, my lord. I meant to—"

"Don't be sorry," said Branford, his tone deliberately rough. "There is a cardinal rule in affairs of honor—never engage in one unless you are quite ready to send the other man to his Maker. Never forget it, if you wish to survive."

Justin regarded him unwaveringly. "I see. And naturally, you always adhere to your own rules."

"I missed."

The corners of Justin's mouth turned up slightly. "No doubt you think me a good many things, my lord, but I would have hoped that one of them would not be a bloody idiot."

Branford couldn't repress the twitch of his own lips. "No," he admitted. "I do not consider you a fool, Chilton."

"Then please do not try to fob me off with such a Banbury tale." His eyes shifted down to his boots and his voice became more tentative. "I don't really understand, sir. Why *did* you miss? We both know you could easily have put a period to my existence if you so chose—and have been well rid of a nuisance to yourself. I cannot help but wonder why you didn't." He hesitated. "I mean, it does not seem as if you should have any reason to care."

Branford looked uncomfortable. He shifted his position against the squabs and went back to staring out the window at the countryside rolling by. Justin had all but given up on getting an answer when the earl finally spoke.

"You have not asked me where we are going," he said abruptly.

"I imagine you will tell me when you see fit to do so, my lord," replied Justin. However he was determined not to let the other matter drop without a last attempt at getting an answer to his question—the fact was, as well as being deucedly curious, he was amazed that someone as cool and self-assured as the earl seemed to have conflicting emotions too. "But you are changing the subject."

Another slight smile pulled at Branford's lips, followed by a sigh.

"You may ask me that question after we have found Alex and I have had a chance to speak with her."

Justin nodded slowly. There was a hint of understanding in his eyes—he had noted the use of his sister's given name, and the nuance of emotion in the earl's tone. "Very well, sir." He considered that the subject had been dropped but after a short time Branford spoke again, almost as if to himself.

"Lord knows, I've acted in a remarkably stupid manner." His hand came up to rub at his temple. "A complete muttonhead in regard to . . ."

He trailed off, shaking his head.

Justin regarded him thoughtfully. "That is hard to believe, sir. You—well, you always seem in such command."

"Any man can be a bloody fool at times. Remember that advice, too." He cleared his throat. "But I hope you will soon accept that my faults concerning your sister have been no more grievous than that."

Justin took his time in answering. "I think that deep inside I've known that all along, my lord. Somehow, I—I believe I can trust you."

"I thank you for that, Chilton," he said softly.

Both of them seemed satisfied to dwell on their own thoughts for a time. The silence had lost its edge of tension. The clatter of the wheels and the sounds of the horses pounding over the country roads were the only reminders that trouble still lay ahead of them.

Justin's expression became serious, his shoulders growing rigid against the soft leather. "Do you really think we can find her? I mean, how do you possibly know where to begin looking?"

"Your father's letter."

"What!"

"I should have given it the attention that Alex wished, then perhaps all of this might have been avoided."

Justin's eyes grew wide.

"Your sister was right," continued Branford. "The letter held the answer to everything. I had just figured it out this morning when you arrived." His fist drove into the palm of his other hand. "I was about to send a warning to Alex. It is Hammerton who is behind all this."

"Hammerton!" exclaimed Justin. "Why ever would he wish to harm either of us? What possible threat are we to a man in his position?"

Branford gave a curt laugh. "That is exactly the crux of it, Chilton. You see, your father, and not John Plainfield, was the rightful Earl of Hammerton. As you are now."

Justin's expression changed from puzzlement to sheer astonishment.

"Alex, with her suspicions aroused by the accidents, was probing a little too close for comfort. It's evident that Hammerton must have had his eye on you for quite awhile. Once it became clear you would be spending time in town, in contact with the *ton*, he no doubt decided he couldn't afford to take a chance that you would stumble onto his secret. If Alex had been a normal female, he would have left her alone." His mouth tightened. "I should have had you tie her to her easel after she went off in the dead of night to a rendezvous arranged by that other note."

"She did *what*?"

Branford colored slightly. "Er, we shall discuss that at a later time as well. Suffice it to say, I was able to extricate her with a minimum amount of damage—the shot merely grazed her shoulder. But you would think it would have knocked enough sense in her not to go haring off a second time."

Justin bit his lip. "I imagine she felt she had no one to turn to. I didn't take her seriously. And as you may well guess, Alex does not back down in the face of trouble, especially when she thinks those she cares about are threatened."

They both exchanged rather guilty looks.

"Even though you know it is Hammerton"—Justin continued after a moment's thought—"how are we ever going to find where he is holding her before this evening?" He gestured toward the rolling fields and stands of oak outside the window. "Why, he could be anywhere!"

Branford steepled his fingers. "Possibly. But I have heard rumors of certain . . . activities that Hammerton and his dissolute cronies like to indulge in occasionally. One of those men is Baron Whitleigh, who is wont to pass his afternoons in White's with a bottle of brandy. With a little encouragement, he found he was able to recall that Hammerton has a hunting box in Burnham Beeches. So we are going to pay him a little visit—I believe vermin are in season."

He made himself a little more comfortable on the seat. "And another thing, Chilton. As we are going to be in each other's pocket for the next while, Branford will do, rather than those incessant 'sirs' and 'my lords'—I am not yet in my dotage."

Justin gave a shy grin. "Yes, sir!"

"Henry?"

Lord Ashton handed his hat and cane to his butler and entered the drawing room.

"My dear, I am so glad you have returned." Lady Ashton's face was clouded with worry. "I have just come from a second visit to Miss Chilton's aunt and have received some very disturbing news. The girl is missing. Lady Beckworth is beside herself, as you can well imagine. From what I gather, a note was delivered to Alex early this morning. She left the house shortly afterward unaccompanied and hasn't been seen since." Unable to contain her agitation, she rose from her seat and began to pace the room. "I was just about to visit Sebastian to inform him of what has occurred—though I fear he is in no condition to do anything about it."

Ashton's face was grim. "You needn't bother. I've just come from White's, where young Whitleigh is in a near state of apoplexy from having Sebastian wave a brace of pistols under his nose earlier this afternoon. Babbled something about a hunting box Hammerton has in Burnham Beeches and couldn't fathom why the devil Sebastian was so interested in it."

"Hammerton? I must say I've never cared for the man—too oily by half." She pursed her lips in thought. "Sebastian must think he has something to do with Alex's disappearance."

A glimmer came to her eyes. She paused, then went back to the sofa and grabbed up her reticule. "The carriage is still outside, I take it?"

"Where are you going?" demanded her husband.

"Not I. We. We are going after them as soon as you fetch your pistols. Sebastian may need our help."

"Now listen here, Cecelia. You are not coming along. It may be dangerous—"

The door slammed shut.

"Bloody hell," muttered Ashton as he hurried after his wife.

The carriage lurched to a stop. Hammerton grabbed Alex by the arm and shoved her roughly toward the door he had flung open. Her foot caught on one of the steps and she fell to the ground. A flash of anger roared through her, as raw as the scrapes on her palms. Rising slowly, she scooped up a handful of dirt and flung it in Hammerton's face as he was dismounting.

"Ahhhggg," he cried, his hands clawing at his eyes which were momentarily blinded by the grit.

Alex turned to run toward a copse of trees she had spotted from the carriage window—and collided smack into a male chest.

"Hold her, you bloody idiot!" roared Hammerton.

Standish's arm came around her. Scratching and kicking proved ineffective, but a well-placed knee to the groin had the desired effect. Free once more, she bolted toward the shelter of the woods. Though she hadn't seen any signs of habitation for miles, perhaps she could lose her captors and find some way of calling off her brother. However her skirted legs proved no match for Hammerton's booted ones.

Shaking her hard enough to rattle her teeth, he bent one of her arms behind her back and marched her back toward where his cousin lay writhing in pain.

"The bitch," moaned Standish, still curled in a fetal position. "I'll make her pay for this. I'll—"

"Later," snarled Hammerton. "We need her untouched until we have her cursed brother in hand." He gave Alex a nasty leer. "It won't be long. Then you may do whatever you like with her."

Leaving Arthur to recover on his own, he propelled Alex toward a small, rustic lodge made of thick timber and masonry. It was surrounded on three sides by a tall, crumbling stone wall. To the left sat a neglected orchard whose unpruned branches dangled over its mossy top. The rutted drive snaked to the right, past the wall, down to a small outbuilding that served as the stable. Hammerton lit a taper as he entered the dank center hall, then pushed her through an open door on one side of a narrow hall. The meager rays of sunlight that managed to penetrate into the room did little to relieve the oppressive feeling of the place. Hammerton paused to light the fire, but even its flames seemed unable to ward off the chill.

"Sit down," ordered Hammerton as he pushed her toward a simple wooden chair. "If you try to escape again, I promise you I will make it very unpleasant for that brother of yours."

Alex's chin went up. "Do with me what you wish. Justin will not be fool enough to fall into your trap, I assure you."

Hammerton gave a nasty laugh. "Of course he will, my dear. Family loyalty runs deep in the greener branches of this family, doesn't it?" The laugh trailed off into a nasty sneer. "And you cannot expect your erstwhile friend Branford to rush to your rescue this time, can you?"

Alex's face must have betrayed some emotion for he laughed again. "Oh yes, that was rather clever of me too, wasn't it? The whole thing, I mean." He lifted a booted leg up on the rough oak table and regarded his well-manicured nails.

"What do you mean?" said Alex in a hoarse whisper.

His look of satisfaction clearly showed how disappointed he would have been had she not asked.

"First of all, I conceived of an ingenious plan to force the three of you back to the country—accidents are so much easier to contrive in such a setting. Knowing the earl's reputation with the ladies, I took advantage of finding him foxed one night at our club and bet him he couldn't mount you. That would have been one bet I wouldn't have minded losing to that arrogant son of a bitch." He shook his head slightly. "It would have worked perfectly. Once he had succeeded, I would have carefully seen to it that word spread throughout the *ton*. You would have been ruined, and the rest of your family with you. Your aunt would have had no choice but to take the two of you back to the country, that is, if she didn't turn you out onto the street."

He looked down at his nails once again. "I cannot fathom why he called the bet off. Apparently it was quite a scene when he stormed in and scratched the wager out of the betting book, announcing that he didn't toy with innocents."

Alex closed her eyes for a moment, feeling slightly sick.

"Hah!" Hammerton went on, his voice becoming more agitated. "Who is he to flaunt a code of honor? Everyone knows he murdered his cousin for the title and got away with it. Why should he be treated with such respect and awe? He isn't nearly as clever as I am!"

"You are quite mad," remarked Alex calmly.

Hammerton pounded his fist into the table. "Am I? The mark of a superior mind is flexibility. When that approach didn't work, I bided my time, waiting for another opportunity. You, with your meddlesome ways, provided another way to get at your brother—and deal with Branford as well. Have you any idea what I planned for the night you came running in response to my note? Even you would have been hard pressed to denounce as a forgery the letter I had written." He chuckled gleefully in recalling the plan. "You would have ended up in the river and all of Society would have heard the sad tale of how Branford seduced and deserted you. Your aunt and brother would have retreated to the country and Branford would be lucky indeed if he were ever received again in polite company. Of course, after a short time, your brother would also have met with an unfortunate accident."

Alex sucked in her breath at the sheer horror of the plan. "Why do you hate him so? What has he done to you?"

"People bow and scrape before him. They fear him, but they respect him, just because of his war record," he said angrily. "Yet I am the one who is truly the clever one. They should look up to me! They should fear and respect me!"

"They respect Lord Branford because he has shown courage and honor. Despite what you say, he is a true gentleman, while you are no better than a toad who has crawled out from under a rock."

He laughed, a malevolent sound that sent a chill through her. "But in the end, you see, I've beaten you all." There was a note of triumph in his voice. "With my careful planning I have outmaneuvered even the hero soldier—it was a stroke of genius, was it not, to become your confidant after turning you against Branford?"

When she didn't speak, he narrowed his eyes. "Well? Answer me!"

"You are a loathsome creature," she said slowly. "And not half so clever as you think. You'll see." She wished she believed the last part of her words.

Hammerton's face turned ugly. "Shut your mouth! With such a shrewish tongue it is no wonder Branford couldn't stomach the idea of taking you to his bed—you have none of the charms that one of your sex should have."

"And you have none of the qualities a gentleman should have. You are not fit to be part of respectable society."

He raised a hand as if to strike her, then appeared to think better of it. "Later," he said, half to himself. Instead, he contented himself with rummaging in a cabinet until he extracted a length of rope. He jerked her to her feet, tied her hands together in front of her, and then shoved her back down in the chair.

"Make yourself comfortable," he sneered. "We have a while before it is time to fetch your dear brother." He turned on his heel and left the room.

The door slammed with a thud. The key turned in the lock. Alex's chin sunk to her chest in despair.

Sykes slowed the carriage. "Looks like we're coming to the place, Cap'n."

"Keep a steady pace," called Branford in a low voice.

He studied the entrance to the grounds of Hammerton's hunting box. The drive was narrow and overgrown, lined on both sides with gnarled elms whose branches intertwined to cast a gloomy shadow over the rutted surface. No building was visible from the main road. In fact, there hadn't been any sign of habitation since passing through a small village five miles back.

After traveling for perhaps another quarter mile, Branford signaled for the carriage to pull over. Sykes guided the horses into a small clearing where a copse of tall bushes would screen them from any other travelers, though so far, the road had been deserted. The earl got out rather stiffly, followed by Justin.

"Keep a sharp eye out," said Branford tersely to Sykes as he thrust his pistols into the pockets of his coat. "Make sure your weapons are primed."

"Aye, they're ready." Sykes cast a glance at Justin, who stood in the earl's shadow, nervously shifting his weight from foot to foot. "Sure you'll not be wanting me to go with ye?" His dubious look implied his assessment of Justin's usefulness. "The lad here could watch the horses."

There was the tiniest of pauses. "No need. I've no doubt Chilton here can handle things well enough."

Justin's face struggled manfully to hide both his gratitude and his apprehension.

Branford went on. "Perhaps you should keep watch on the drive. Though I don't expect it, we wouldn't want any unwanted visitors."

Sykes nodded in agreement.

Branford turned to Justin. "Let's be off."

He moved into the trees with a lithe quickness that had Justin nearly breaking into a run in order to keep up. With nary a hesitation, the earl threaded his way through the woods until it gave way to the grounds of the hunting box. They were on the edge of a small clearing, behind the building that served as the stable. Branford motioned for Justin to pause behind the cover of a bushy hemlock.

"How did you find . . ." whispered Justin.

Branford pressed a finger to his lips and watched for any

activity. The sounds of someone moving around inside the stalls were clearly audible but there was not a soul in sight. The earl removed the pistols from his coat and wordlessly handed one to Justin. Motioning the young man to follow, he loped across the open space, then quickly pressed himself up against the rough stone of the back wall. When no alarm was sounded, he began inching his way around the building to gain a view of the doorway.

A figure appeared, wrestling with a section of leather harness and paying no heed to his surroundings as a string of curses escaped his lips. It was only when the cold steel muzzle of the pistol pressed against his neck that his head jerked up, eyes wide with terror.

"B-B-Bran—"

"Quiet!" snarled the earl, shoving the other man back into the dark interior of the stable. Standish dropped the harness and grabbed at one of the stall doors to steady his quaking legs.

"Well, well. I should have hazarded a guess you'd be involved in this." Branford's expression became grim. "Where is she?"

Standish appeared speechless with fright. Branford pressed the muzzle even harder against the pulsing vein in his neck and cocked the weapon. It made an audible click, which seemed to have the desired effect.

"In . . . the lodge." His head nodded convulsively toward the high wall hiding the other building from their view.

"Who is with her?"

"Just Hammerton." Standish wet his lips. "I swear, he forced me . . . I wanted nothing to do with—"

"Save your groveling for the magistrate," said Branford harshly.

Justin spoke for the first time. "Is she . . . unhurt?"

Standish could only nod, his lips were trembling so badly.

The earl regarded him with a look of utter disdain. "Chilton, find some rope to bind the swine."

Justin found a length hanging from one of the beams. "Shall I gag him as well? He might raise an alarm as soon as we leave."

Branford's brows came together. "Quite right." He appeared to be considering the matter when suddenly he spun on his heel, his arm a mere blur in the dim light. The fist connected with a solid crack to Standish's chin and the man dropped to the ground, senseless as a sack of grain.

Justin gave a low whistle of appreciation. "I say, neatly done, my lor—Branford."

The earl allowed himself a slight smile. "A campaign on the Peninsula teaches one certain things that come in useful in situations such as these. Hurry and let us bind him anyway, though I doubt he shall be in any state to trouble us for quite some time."

They made short work of it, leaving Standish locked inside one of the stalls, then stealthily approached the wall surrounding the lodge.

"Damnation!" muttered Branford.

Justin looked questioningly at him.

"I should like to avoid dropping down in full view of Hammerton—there is no telling how he might react . . ." He left the sentence unfinished. "We cannot tell from here how the house is situated."

He thought for a moment, then began to move around to where the gnarled apple trees hanging over the top of the wall afforded some cover as well as a means for scaling the height. Stopping at one of the sturdier trunks, he stripped off his coat, stuck the pistol between his teeth, and began to climb. Once on the top, he sprawled flat on his stomach and slithered ahead over the moss and twigs for several yards.

After surveying the area for several minutes, he motioned for Justin to come up as well.

They were opposite the side of the hunting box. A squat, two-story structure, it had only a few small windows facing in their direction, and those appeared to have their curtains drawn. Satisfied, Branford swung his legs over the side and dropped to the ground with barely a sound. His brow damp with perspiration, his breathing ragged from all the physical effort, he paused by a thick oak, leaning up against its sturdy bulk for a moment to marshal his strength.

Justin came up behind him. "Are you all right?" he whispered, noting with concern that a small patch of crimson was beginning to stain the earl's shirt.

Branford nodded curtly. "I hope your sister will be content to putter in the gardens of Riverton and devote her energies to her exquisite paintings when she is safe and sound—I am getting too old for this," he muttered through gritted teeth.

Justin made as if to say something, then shut his mouth. Despite the gravity of the situation, a true smile flashed across his face for a moment as he realized the import of the earl's words.

Branford took one more deep breath then edged noiselessly toward the lodge. From the vantage point of the timbered corner he ascertained that no one was outside and again motioned Justin to join him. Ducking low to pass underneath the main windows, the two men gained the front door. It was slightly ajar, but they could hear no sounds from within.

Branford ventured a quick look inside, then withdrew to consider the next course of action. After a moment's consideration, he indicated to Justin to stay where he was, then pantomimed that he would enter the building alone. Justin looked as if he meant to argue, but something in Branford's eyes made him reconsider. Pressing his lips together, he nodded a silent assent. With an answering nod, Branford cocked his weapon and slid into the shadows.

Even now, Hammerton was paying little heed to her. He had returned to the room a short time after leaving it and had made no further efforts at conversation. Without so much as a glance in her direction, he had fetched a bottle of brandy and pulled his own chair up to the long table. Turned sideways, his profile silhouetted in the fading afternoon sun, he seemed content to stare into his glass with the satisfied smirk she had come to hate.

Tallying up his fortune and his lands no doubt, Alex thought bitterly. And gloating over his future, which now seemed safe at least. At least he had remained silent and she didn't have to listen to any more of his boasting. Yet she wasn't sure which was worse—having to listen to his chilling revelations or having to dwell on her own damnable stupidity.

She bit her lip until she nearly drew blood. From the first, she had felt she could trust Branford, no matter what other people said about his reputation. Why had she let her head overrule her heart? Why had she let reason banish intuition? He must think her just like all the rest now. Of course, he hadn't helped matters—why the devil hadn't he explained?

Her throat tightened. Because she had not allowed him. A simple yes or no, my lord, she had demanded. So his own honor had demanded that he tell the unvarnished truth. She blinked away tears. How could he ever forgive her for not believing in him? And that wasn't the worst of it, she had to admit. A good part of her anger had stemmed from the fact that she had been unsure of herself, afraid that she could never be as glamorous or alluring as his other amours. So she had lashed out at him. It had been petty. It had been wrong.

Not that it mattered much now, but she wished somehow she could tell him . . . Suddenly she felt the knots were beginning to loosen from the constant twistings of her hands. Though her wrists were raw from the rough hemp, she could now slip her hands free. Banishing her regrets, she forced herself to stay alert, to stay watchful.

Things weren't over yet.

The chair scraped back on the plank floor. Hammerton consulted a pocketwatch and got to his feet. Alex noted with some dismay that he had limited his libations to one small glass of the spirits. Unfortunately, he was no fool in that regard.

"It is time for us to leave, dear cousin," he said as he slipped the watch back in his waistcoat pocket. "Arthur should have the carriage ready and we wouldn't want to keep your brother waiting, would we?"

Chapter Ten

"I think not, Hammerton."

Hammerton spun around, mouth agape.

"Sebastian!" cried Alex as she shot up from the chair.

Branford stepped deliberately into the room, pistol fully extended, pointed square at Hammerton's chest. "Are you all right, my dear?" he asked, never taking his eyes from the other man.

"Y—yes," stammered Alex. "But how did you ever—"

"Your father's letter," answered Branford. "I finally gave it the attention I should have when you first asked me to look at it. If I only had—well, I'm sorry. I should have prevented this."

"*You* are sorry," exclaimed Alex. "I—" She suddenly noticed the ugly red splotch seeping through the fabric of Branford's muddied and disheveled shirt. "My God, you are hurt!"

Instinctively she took a step toward him.

"Alex! No!" he began. But it was too late.

For a brief second, she came between Hammerton and Branford's pistol. It was all the time the other man needed. His arm shot around Alex's neck, dragging her right up against his body to shield him from any further threat. In a flash, he whipped out a knife he had hidden in his pocket and pressed it up against the side of her throat with enough pressure to draw a bead of crimson.

"Put the gun down on the table!" he shouted.

Branford hesitated.

"Don't, Sebastian," said Alex. "You know he'll only kill us both. Put a bullet in the monster."

"Shut up, you bitch!" He shook her roughly, causing Branford to take an involuntary step toward him.

"Stop! Put it down," he cried again, his grip tightening around her throat even more. "I swear, I'll cut her throat if you don't by the time I count to three—and I shall enjoy every second of it." The wildness of his expression made it clear the threat was not an idle one. "One!"

Branford's eyes narrowed, the only sign of emotion on his face. For the first time he took note of the darkening bruise on Alex's cheek."

"Two!"

"You know, you have just signed your own death warrant, Hammerton," he said softly as he lowered the weapon and set it skidding halfway down the table.

It was still out of Hammerton's reach. Even so, he relaxed his hold on Alex, letting the knife fall slightly away from her skin. Sure of his victory, he couldn't help but gloat.

"Hah! You see, I *am* smarter than all of you," he crowed. "I've beaten you, by God, Branford. I've beaten you in the battle of wits and now I'm going to shoot you down like the dog you are."

"Is that so?" inquired Branford with no trace of emotion in his voice. He seemed to want to keep Hammerton talking. "Why exactly do you hate me so?"

As he spoke, he moved slightly forward.

Hammerton didn't notice, so caught up in his rantings was he. "Everyone thinks you are the clever one for having saved Wellington. Any idiot can appear a hero in war. You're not clever, merely lucky. *I'm* the clever one. People should look at me with respect in their eyes, not you. Why you—you are nothing but a murderer!"

"Rather the pot calling the kettle black, wouldn't you say?" said Branford dryly. He inched another step closer.

"Oh that." He smirked. "Was I to let an eccentric old man take away what I had worked for all my life?" He slanted a quick glance at Alex. "So the old codger did manage to warn you? I don't see how—I climbed down to the wreck and checked his pockets and belongings quite thoroughly. And I inquired at every possible place he could have posted a letter."

"Not thoroughly enough, it seems," said Branford, saving Alex from having to answer her tormentor. "He left a letter of warning in one of his books."

Hammerton furrowed his brow. "There was nothing but scientific gibberish."

"It was a code." Branford gave a slight smile. "I'm afraid the eccentric old man managed to outwit you."

Anger flashed in Hammerton's eyes. "Hardly! The fool is dead. And so will all of you be in a short time, including that sapskull of a brother of yours. For all the trouble you've given me I shall be well rid of a tiresome nuisance." He gave Alex another shake. "I am protecting what is rightfully mine! *I* am the true Earl of Hammerton." The hand that held the knife jabbed at the air to punctuate the point.

Alex saw her chance. Her hands slipped out of the loosened bonds. One shoved Hammerton into the table while the other shot out for the pistol. Hammerton recovered and moved nearly as quickly toward the weapon, but she managed to knock it away from him and twist out of his reach. His arm dealt her a resounding blow as she escaped his grasp, but he wasted no time coming after her. He lunged for the gun.

Branford moved at the same instant. The two of them came together, grappling for the pistol that lay so tantalizingly close. The struggle went on for what seemed like ages, the two bodies intertwined, first one on top, then the other. It appeared that Branford had the advantage, with his superior size and skill, but his strength was ebbing from all the previous exertions. Hammerton managed to free one hand and land a vicious blow to Branford's injured side. It doubled him over, sending him to his knees and allowing Hammerton to grab the pistol. He jumped back, out of arm's reach.

"It is *you* who are the dead man," he sneered as Branford painfully dragged himself to his feet.

He raised the pistol and with a wicked laugh took dead aim at Branford's heart.

A shot rang out.

Alex screamed.

For an instant, no one moved. Then Hammerton lowered his eyes, an incredulous look on his face as he watched his white shirtfront slowly turn red.

"No! It can't be . . ." he said faintly as he crumpled to the floor.

Branford brushed some of the dregs of leaves and moss from his sleeve. "Thank you, Justin. I'm relieved to see that your aim left nothing to chance on this occasion."

Alex staggered to her feet, not quite believing that Branford was still standing. With a small cry, she rushed across the room and flung her arms around him, holding him very tightly and burying her face against the familiar warmth of his shoulder.

"I thought that monster would pull the trigger, and I'd never have a chance to tell you . . ." Her voice wavered. "W-w-what happened?"

His cheek came to rest against her hair and his hand

stroked the long, curling locks that had come loose in the struggle. "Fortunately, my dear, your brother has become an excellent shot."

Alex picked up her head to see Justin's figure framed in the doorway, the smoking pistol held calmly by his side. "Oh, Justin, thank God, you are safe! I was so afraid that you would let Hammerton lure you into his grasp."

"Though you sometimes consider me little more than a child, I should hope you wouldn't think me addlepated enough to fall into such an obvious trap." He grinned. "Besides, I knew you'd ring such a peal over my head if I got us both sent to our Maker that I couldn't even consider the possibility. So I"—he looked rather shyly at Branford—"I went to the one person I trusted could help us."

"I am no magician," said the earl. "It was your father's letter. I finally deciphered the code and discovered it was Hammerton who was the villain behind all this. Remember those little symbols? The hatchets, you called them. Hammers, really. How blind can I have been? I might have spared you this ordeal."

Alex looked from Branford to her brother and then back to the earl. Suddenly she burst into tears.

"Oh dear, I never cry," she managed to croak between sobs.

Branford merely pressed her to his chest and waited wordlessly until her shoulders stopped heaving.

"Really," she sniffed. "I am usually never so weak as to become such a veritable watering pot."

"Alex," murmured Branford as he gently brushed away a tear from her bruised cheek. "You do not have to carry the entire weight of the world on your own, very capable shoulders any longer."

She looked up at his face. It was deathly pale beneath the dirt and sweat, and a trickle of dried blood had formed at the corner of his mouth where another of Hammerton's blows had connected. But his eyes sparkled with a warmth that sent fire throughout her entire being. She reached up and ran her hand lightly along the line of his jaw.

"Oh, Sebastian," she whispered.

His head came down toward hers.

The front door was thrown open with a bang and there was the clatter of footsteps in the hallway, followed by the sound of familiar voices.

"Damnation!" muttered Branford. Then he kissed her anyway. Long, hard, possessively.

Justin, the grin still on his face, reached out and pulled the door firmly shut.

At least for a brief interlude, they had only each other.

Moments later, Lord Ashton and Sykes burst in, pistols at the ready, followed by a very determined Lady Ashton brandishing her parasol like a saber.

"Sorry, Cap'n." Sykes lowered his pistol and tried to repress a grin at the earl's current situation. "When I couldn't convince his lordship and her ladyship to stop, I figured I better come along as well."

Ashton surveyed the body on the floor and Branford with Alex wrapped in an intimate embrace.

"You see, my dear," he said rather smugly, "I told you Sebastian would have things well in hand without any help from us."

"A little too well in hand," she retorted. "Sebastian!" she added sharply, turning to face the earl. "What is the meaning of this, may I ask, taking advantage of a young lady behind closed doors?"

"I think you know very well what it means, Cecelia," he answered dryly. "But you could at least allow me to pay my addresses without an audience."

"Of course you may—in due time." She smiled sweetly.

"Just so we all understand each other. I have noticed that Mr. Chilton is holding a pistol and I wouldn't want there to be any more misunderstandings."

Branford chuckled. "I think Chilton knows by now that my intentions are entirely honorable."

To her dismay, Alex found herself coloring to the roots. "But Lady Ashton, it's not what you think. Sebas—Lord Branford should not be forced—I mean, he doesn't want to mar—"

"We shall discuss that in the carriage ride back to town," interrupted Branford.

To her own surprise, Alex fell silent without an argument.

Branford turned to Ashton. "How did you manage to track us down, Henry?"

"I'm afraid half of White's could do so if they wished. Odds are fifty-fifty on whether Whitleigh will recover."

"Yes, well, I suppose the gossips will have more than enough fodder for their hungry tongues after today." He glanced at Hammerton's lifeless form. "Would you and Chilton—or should I say, the real Lord Hammerton—be kind enough to summon the magistrates and settle matters here. There is another cur out in the stables that must be dealt with as well. I would like to attend to . . . other things."

Ashton regarded Justin, and then the pistol in his hand. "I take it, Chilton, we have you to thank for keeping Sebastian from sticking his spoon in the wall today?"

A glimmer of a smile came to Justin's countenance. "I received some very wise advice about putting pistols to more honorable use, sir. And it is I who owe both you and Lady Ashton thanks. Without your counsel, I fear things would have turned out very differently."

Ashton's reserve finally melted away. "The Earl of Hammerton is it? Hmmm. I like the sound of it, young man. I think you will be a credit to the title." He grinned at Branford. "I think his lordship and I would be happy to straighten things up here. I shall send my driver for the authorities right away."

Branford nodded his thanks. "I should like Sykes to drive Alex and me back to town as soon as possible. She has had enough excitement for the day, and I'm sure her aunt is sick with worry."

Ashton nodded. "No doubt. Pray, don't worry about a thing." He repressed a little chuckle. "Have a most pleasant—and unexciting—journey."

"Miss Chilton," called Lady Ashton. "I look forward to some very long, comfortable cozes with you. I believe we have much to discuss—I consider myself something of an expert on the matrimonial state."

Ashton rolled his eyes. "I fear, my poor friend, you have no idea what you are getting yourself into."

Branford tightened his arm around Alex. "Oh, but indeed I do, Henry. Indeed I do."

Branford settled his bruised and weary body into the carriage seat with a deep sigh. Next to him, Alex sat silently, her gaze averted out the coach window. Now, with the heat of danger subsided, he felt strangely tentative, unsure of himself. What if she truly didn't wish to . . . But he remembered Cecelia's advice and knew he must take courage and plunge on, regardless of the uncertainty.

He cleared his throat. "Alex. We must clarify a few things."

She turned warily toward him.

"First of all, about that damnable bet—"

"I know. Hammerton couldn't resist telling me about it." Her eyes fell to her feet. "How . . ."

He held his breath, waiting for her to go on.

"How can you ever forgive me for not believing in you?" she said in a wavering voice.

He dared to breathe again.

"I mean," she continued, "I thought I understood what I saw in your eyes that—that night, but afterward you seemed so cool, so distant. It made me think perhaps you regretted what had happened between us. And then you left without so much as a word."

"You never received my letter?"

She shook her head.

His mouth compressed in a tight line. "Hammerton again. I remember now that his carriage was outside the club." He shook his head. "No wonder you thought me the worst sort of blackguard." A deep sigh escaped his lips. "But it is I who should wonder whether you can ever forgive me. I was distant that night because, well, it frightened me that I could care so much for someone else. I had sworn to myself I would never let that happen again."

"It isn't so bad to care, is it? Would you truly have wished not to have loved your cousin? Of course the chance of pain is there. But without it there can be no happiness, or warmth or friendship."

"Just as it isn't so bad to realize you don't have to solve everyone's problems for them—it can be nice to have a shoulder to lean on." His hand stole around hers. "I think you would like Riverton very much, my love. The gardens are magnificent and you can fill the rooms with your wonderful paintings. For you know, I trust, that I would never interfere with your passions—though I should hope they would include me."

She leaned over and kissed him. "Can you doubt it? And I have the first painting ready—your hibiscus."

He returned the kiss. "I hope you shall not make me work quite as hard for all the rest."

They both laughed softly and then Branford gathered her in his arms.

"Alex, my love. My life would be colorless without you. Will you marry me?"

Her heart soared. She stroked her thumb along the line of his jaw. "Yes," she whispered.

He captured her lips before she could say anything more.

"Sebastian, you are hurt. A man in your condition should . . ." she managed to say a few minutes later.

"A man in my condition needs immediate attention," he murmured as his lips traced a path down the curve of her neck.

"A man in your condition needs to rest and regain his strength," she countered.

"I suppose you are quite right, my love, seeing as the special license I have in my pocket will allow us to be married tomorrow." A twinkle came to his eye. "Rest assured that I intend to be fully recovered in time for our wedding night."